DANCING WITH
DEAD MEN

James Reasoner

DANCING WITH
DEAD MEN

Dancing With Dead Men
Copyright © August 2013 by James Reasoner
Cover Design: L. J. Washburn
Cover Image: shutterstock_22965

1.

Christmas Eve, 1873

The killing had stopped for the holidays. For months the two rival mining syndicates, the Rimfire on one side and the Aldena on the other, had been battling, each side blaming the other – correctly, as it happened – for the rash of robberies, sabotage, and outright murder that had plagued the area around Aspen Creek, Montana Territory.

But tonight, the night before the holiest day of the year, hostilities had ceased. For one night, the war over the gold fields had been put aside, and everyone from the area, townspeople, miners, and ranchers alike, had come together in the Aspen Creek town hall for the annual Christmas dance. The weather had even cooperated. It was cold, but not too cold for late December in Montana Territory, and only a light dusting of snow lay on the ground.

Inside the town hall, the air was hot and stifling. The heat came from the pot-bellied stoves in the corners and also from the several hundred people who had crowded into the building for the festivities.

Logan Handley didn't care much for the heat. A few beads of sweat had popped out on his forehead. He had been sick with a fever recently, and even though he seemed to be over it, he didn't feel like he had recovered completely.

A tall, lean man with close-cropped sandy hair, Logan was better dressed than most of the men in the hall. His frock coat, vest, and string tie would have been fashionable even back east. His lone concessions to Western fashion were the high-topped black boots he wore and the flat-crowned black hat with a silver band that hung on one of the hat trees near the hall's entrance.

He paused at the table on one side of the crowded room to pick up a cup of punch. Before the night was over, somebody would spike that punch, more than likely, but for now it was innocent enough, and Logan enjoyed the cool sweetness as he took a sip.

"Well, lookee there. Standin' around and drinkin' punch like he ain't a cold-blooded killer."

Logan had a pretty good idea who had spoken, but he looked around to be sure. He nodded to the stocky, walrus-mustached man and said, "Merry Christmas, Marshal."

"Maybe it will be, if you hired guns'll behave yourselves," Marshal Floyd Mahaffey said. The badge he wore as city marshal of Aspen Creek gleamed on the lapel of his brown tweed suit coat.

Logan had the cup of punch in his right hand, a cautious habit since he was left-handed. He moved his left hand in a graceful gesture and said, "Do you see me wearing a gun?"

"Not right now," Mahaffey admitted. "I'll bet it's out there in one of the baskets, though."

Well, that much was true, thought Logan. He had unbuckled the black leather shell belt and attached holster with its new .45 caliber Colt Single Action Army revolver and left them in one of the baskets that had been set out on chairs in the foyer. A couple of the marshal's deputies, each armed with a shotgun, stood beside those baskets and made sure that every man who came into the town hall deposited his weapons in one of them before entering. Those guns could only be reclaimed when a fellow left the dance.

The deputies weren't exactly diligent in their duty, though. Logan had a .41 caliber over-and-under derringer in his vest pocket, and he would have bet good money it wasn't the only hide-out gun in the hall tonight.

But as long as nobody used any of those hidden weapons, things would remain peaceful. The musicians sawed on their fiddles, people danced and sang Christmas carols and drank punch, young men and women flirted with each other, kids ran around and got underfoot. Everything was as normal as it could be, and that was a refreshing change for Logan.

For men such as him, normal was lonely trails, smoky saloons, squalid cribs . . . and unmarked, unmourned graves.

"John Purcell appears to be havin' a good time tonight," Mahaffey went on. His dislike for gunmen meant it cost him an obvious effort to be civil to the likes of Logan Handley, but he made that effort.

Logan nodded as his eyes sought out Purcell. The local superintendent of the Rimfire Mining Syndicate – and as such, Logan's employer – was dancing with his wife Bedelia. Over on the other side of the room, Clete Barrows, who ran the Aldena, danced with *his* wife. The two bitter enemies determinedly ignored each other while at the same time making sure as much space as possible separated them. That was wise, Logan thought. An accidental bump on the dance floor might shatter the fragile holiday truce.

"John deserves to have a good time," Logan said. "All that mischief by the Aldena has put a lot of pressure on him. Rimfire's owners don't care what obstacles he has to overcome. All that matters to them is production."

Mahaffey let out a disgusted snort.

"Don't talk to me about what Barrows' men have been doin'. You Rimfire men have been makin' life hell for his operation, too. If there was room in the town cemetery, I'd say all of you oughta just go ahead and kill each other and be done with it."

Logan smiled faintly and took another sip of the punch.

"It's Christmas Eve, Marshal. No killing tonight."

Mahaffey made another disgusted noise, shook his head, and started to turn away. He paused to look back at Logan and said, "I don't see your pard Meadows here."

Logan stiffened. He said, "Jim Meadows is no pard of mine. You know that."

Mahaffey shrugged.

"He may work for Barrows while you work for Purcell, but you and him are the same stripe, I'm thinkin'."

The lawman's stumpy legs carried him into the crowd. Logan looked down into the red liquid remaining in his cup and frowned. He didn't like being told that he was the same sort as Jim Meadows, but he supposed it was true, at least in a basic sense. Both of them hired out their guns to whoever offered the biggest payoff.

And they had never been too careful about picking sides, either. There was no moral high ground to claim in this dispute between the Rimfire and the Aldena. It had been the same in other places, other times, when disputes boiled over into gunplay and bloodshed. There had even been a few instances when Logan and Jim Meadows had found themselves riding for the same side.

Logan wanted to call Mahaffey back and insist to the marshal that he and Meadows were different, that Meadows was a snake-blooded killer while he, Logan, at least had a few scruples.

But he couldn't, not really.

His stomach clenched. He set the unfinished punch aside. He couldn't choke down the rest of it. If he did, it might come right back up, and he didn't want to ruin the dance by getting sick in front of everybody.

What the marshal had said about Jim Meadows not being here nagged at Logan's brain. To get his mind off how bad he felt, he looked around the room. Sure enough, he didn't see Meadows anywhere, and that *was* a little surprising. Meadows was a darkly handsome man. He would have been quite popular with Aspen Creek's single ladies tonight and wouldn't have had any problem finding partners for every dance. Logan rubbed his chin and thought.

Whatever Meadows was doing, it had to be something pretty important to keep him away from the dance. And there was a good-sized shipment of bullion in the vault in the Rimfire office down the street, waiting to be shipped out in a couple of days. John Purcell had assigned a couple of men to guard the gold, but that wouldn't mean much to Jim Meadows. He wouldn't let two men keep him from what he wanted.

Two *normal* men, Logan amended. *He* should have been one of the guards, but Purcell hadn't given him the job because he'd been sick and also because Purcell wanted him on hand here at the town hall just in case any trouble broke out at the dance. The more Logan pondered Meadows' absence, though, the more it bothered him.

He headed for the foyer and along the way plucked his hat from the hat tree where it hung.

9

"Leavin', Handley?" one of Mahaffey's deputies asked him as he paused beside the baskets.

"For now," Logan replied as he reached into the basket and picked up his coiled gunbelt and holstered revolver.

"You come back in, you'll have to give up your gun again."

"I know that." Logan buckled on the belt. The Colt's weight felt good on his hip. He had packed an iron for so long that not wearing one threw him off-balance.

He took a long black overcoat lined with sheepskin from a hook and shrugged into it, then stepped outside and went down the half-dozen steps from the building's porch to the ground. The cold air washed over his face. He enjoyed its bracing bite. Stars sparkled in the sky. The storm that had dusted the area with snow had moved on during the day.

Aspen Creek was a good-sized settlement with a business district six blocks long and a number of residences around it. As the supply center not only for the gold fields but also for several large cattle ranches, normally it was a bustling place. Tonight, however, it was quiet and peaceful as Logan moved along the boardwalk toward the headquarters of the Rimfire Mining Syndicate, located in a one-story brick building between the bank and the assay office.

By the time Logan reached the building, the sweat had dried on his forehead and his stomach had settled down. He told himself that he was borrowing trouble even by coming down here. Nothing had happened, or there would have been a commotion. The guards John Purcell had left here were good, tough, competent men.

But would they be a match for Jim Meadows? That question nagged at Logan's mind.

As he came up to the mining syndicate office, he saw a light through the front window, a lamp turned down low by the looks of it. Nothing unusual about that. The guards would want to have some light. Logan tried to look through the window but couldn't really make anything out. He thumbed his hat back and cupped his hands around his eyes to improve his vision.

His breath caught in his throat as he spotted part of a man's booted foot sticking out from behind a desk. He could tell from the way the boot was turned that the man was lying on the floor, and he knew that couldn't be right.

With his left hand on the butt of his Colt, Logan hurried into the dark, narrow passage between the office building and the bank. He didn't have a key to the front door, but he had one that would open the back door. Not many people did: him, John Purcell, Purcell's private secretary, and the syndicate's chief clerk.

Logan didn't need the key, though. When he reached the rear door, he found the lock busted. That confirmed his hunch about something being wrong. He slid the revolver from its holster and moved soundlessly into the building.

Almost immediately, he tripped, and when he put his right hand down to steady himself he touched something wet and sticky. He moved his hand and the back of it brushed against the thing he had stumbled against. A body, of course. Had to be one of the guards. Logan rested his hand on the man's chest, found more drying blood but no heartbeat, no rise and fall of breath. The man was dead.

He felt certain the other guard was, too. Whatever Meadows was up to, he wouldn't leave witnesses behind.

Logan straightened and moved along the hallway. In his mind he could see what had happened. Meadows had made a little noise breaking into the building, and one of the guards had come back here to see what it was about. Meadows had killed him, then jumped the other guard and disposed of him, too. Meadows might already be gone.

But he might still be in here, too, and if he was, Logan intended to make sure he answered for murdering those two men.

The bullion was locked up in the vault. Meadows wouldn't have the combination. Logan himself didn't have it. So how did Meadows think he could get to the gold, if that was what he was after?

Light spilled through the open doorway of Purcell's private office. The vault lay behind that room. Logan moved forward until he could see into the front office where the clerks worked. The second guard, the man whose boot he had spotted through the window, lay behind one of the desks with a pool of blood around his head. Logan could see his sightlessly staring eyes and the gaping wound in his throat. Meadows had cut the guards' throats. That was why there hadn't been any gunshots to alert the town that something was wrong.

Logan eased up to the corner of the lighted doorway. As he held the Colt ready for action, he risked a look. He could see through Purcell's office to the door of the vault room. Meadows crouched in front of the vault door. He had fastened a bundle of dynamite to it and attached a long fuse to the cylinders. As Logan watched, Meadows took a turnip watch from his pocket, flipped it open, and checked the time.

Logan pointed the Colt at Meadows' back, eared back the hammer, and said, "Got an appointment you're late for, Jim?"

2.

He had to give Meadows credit for having cool nerves. The gunman hunkered back on his heels in front of the vault door and looked over his shoulder.

"Thought you'd be down at the dance, Handley," he said. "It's Christmas Eve."

"Yeah, I know. It looks like you're about to celebrate, too." Logan shook his head. "How in the world did you think you'd get away with it? A blast big enough to wreck that door will shake the whole town. You can't carry off enough bullion to make it worth your while before fifty men are here to stop you."

"Well, that might be true," Meadows drawled as he smiled faintly, "if not for the fact that everybody in town is gonna be pretty busy in a few minutes." He was still holding the watch, and as he snapped it closed, he went on, "You see, one of my men is lighting the fuse on a box of dynamite underneath the town hall right about now."

The chill that went through Logan at those words was much colder than the air outside. The town hall was set up several feet on pilings, and he knew it was possible somebody could crawl under there with a box of dynamite, especially from the back of the building where nobody was likely to be around.

Of course, Meadows could be bluffing. But he had checked his watch when he didn't know Logan was watching him, which meant the time was important to him. If Meadows was telling the truth and was able to time this blast with the one that destroyed the town hall, nobody would hear it. Anyway, even if they did, the other explosion would be so devastating that nobody would care what might be happening inside the Rimfire offices.

"You'll kill hundreds of people," Logan said. His voice sounded hollow and faraway in his ears. Blood pounded inside his skull with every beat of his heart. "Your own boss is in there!"

"After tonight I won't be working for Barrows and Aldena any more," Meadows said.

It was true. There was enough gold in the vault so that Meadows would never have to sell his gun again. He could head for some place like Mexico and live out his days in luxury.

Every instinct in Logan's body shouted out to him that Meadows was telling the truth. Involuntarily, he turned away, thinking that he had to get back to the town hall and warn everyone at the dance. He had done plenty of things in his life he wasn't proud of, but he couldn't stand by and allow Meadows to murder all those people.

It was almost the worst thing he could have done, and he realized that a second later when Meadows surged up from his crouch, leaped across the room with the speed of a striking snake, and tackled him.

The collision knocked Logan off his feet. Pain shot through him as he hit the floor, but he hung on to his gun and swung it at Meadows' head. He should have just blown a hole through the gunman and then raced back to the town hall, but it was too late for that.

Meadows ducked the blow and hammered punches into Logan's body and head. Logan heaved himself off the floor and threw Meadows to the side. He tried to bring his gun to bear again, but Meadows lashed out with his right leg and the heel of his boot caught Logan on the wrist. This time he couldn't maintain his grip on the Colt. It slipped from his fingers and flew across the room.

Meadows came up on one knee and clawed his gun from its holster. Logan knew the man wouldn't hesitate to kill him. His hand dipped into his vest pocket and came up with the derringer. It cracked a split-second before Meadows fired. Blood flew as Meadows went down. The shot he squeezed off went well over Logan's head and slammed into the wall.

Logan knew he had hit Meadows in the head. He hoped the gunman was dead. Either way, he was running out of time. Meadows' accomplice, whoever he was, had to have lit the fuse on the dynamite under the town hall by now.

Logan scrambled to his feet and dashed out of Purcell's office. He headed for the front door, lowered his shoulder, and crashed into it. The jamb splintered and the door flew open. Logan stumbled onto the boardwalk and turned toward the town hall. Somebody up there must have heard the shots from the Rimfire office, because several men stood on the porch and stared down the street toward Logan. He started running toward them and waved his arms to get their attention.

He had gone only a few steps when pain worse than any he had ever felt in his life exploded through him.

The agony was so bad it knocked him off his feet. His momentum carried him forward and he slammed down onto the boardwalk with such force that he somersaulted off into the street. He landed in the snow and mud.

At first he thought he'd been shot. He had experienced such smashing impacts before. He knew how the sudden pain gave way to numbness like he was beginning to experience now.

While he could still move, he tried to get his hands under him and push himself back to his feet so he could run to the town hall. His right arm moved, but his left didn't. Logan realized to his horror that he couldn't even feel it. It was like something had come along and sheared that arm off at the shoulder.

But he still had one good arm, so he used it to brace himself as he struggled to climb upright. As soon as he put weight on his right leg, though, it crumpled and went out from under him.

Left arm, right leg . . . That didn't make sense. Unless he'd been shot twice, once in each place. But he hadn't heard any shots, and he was sure Jim Meadows had been either unconscious or dead when he rushed out of the mining syndicate offices.

Logan raised his head and looked toward the town hall. The men who had come out onto the porch had turned their backs and started inside the building. He realized they had seen him wallowing around in the street and decided that he was drunk. That would explain the shots, too, since plenty of men had been known to get liquored up and fire a gun into the air, especially on holidays.

"No," he groaned. "Get out . . . of there!"

The men couldn't hear him. They were too far away.

Logan heard something else: hoofbeats. Somebody was riding away from the town hall in a hurry. That made sense. Anybody who just lit the fuse to a whole box of dynamite would want to put some distance between themselves and the explosives as fast as possible!

Logan gritted his teeth and groaned again. His left arm still flopped uselessly at his side and his right leg was almost as limp, but when he got the leg under him this time and carefully pushed himself up, he was able to balance on it and his good left leg. He started hobbling toward the town hall. He couldn't risk moving too fast, because if he did he would fall down again.

But if he moved too slow the building would go up in a huge blast and everyone inside would be killed. Men, women, children, all gone in a flash of noise and fire . . .

Logan kept moving. One foot in front of the other, he told himself.

As he walked unsteadily toward the town hall, he used his right hand to check for bullet wounds. He didn't find any, which made no sense. What else could have knocked him down and crippled him like this?

He didn't have time to think about the answer. He was closer now, close enough to start yelling in a raspy voice. He shouted, "Dynamite! Get out, get out!"

The doors were closed. He heard music through them, bright, merry Christmas carols. The people inside would be dancing, he thought, dancing with no idea what was really right under their feet.

"Hey! Hey in there! Dynamite!"

One of the doors opened, and a familiar stocky figure stepped out, silhouetted by the light behind him. Marshal Floyd Mahaffey called, "Who the hell's doin' all that caterwaulin' out here?" He paused, then said, "Handley? Is that you? What's wrong with you, man? You drunk?"

Logan was almost there. The world spun crazily around him, the beat of his pulse inside his skull was like an enormous drum, and when he tried to respond to the marshal's questions a fit of coughing seized him. Finally he gasped, "Dynamite . . . under building! Get everybody . . . out!"

Mahaffey roared a curse and ducked back into the hall. Logan heard shouts and screams as the place erupted in panic. He had worried that Mahaffey wouldn't believe him, but obviously the marshal didn't want to take that chance. More men appeared in the doorway as they tried to stampede out of the place, but they hung up and got stuck there as they struggled with each other in their fear.

Like a herd of spooked horses getting in each other's way, the people inside the town hall would never be able to get out before the explosion went off, not all of them, anyway. Logan didn't know how much time was left, but it couldn't be much. He had to try to stop the blast.

Dropping to the ground was no problem. He'd been fighting not to fall down for the past few minutes. He let himself go, sprawled on his belly, and began to drag and push himself under the building, using his one good arm and one good leg. He crawled between the nearest pilings and looked around as frantic footsteps pounded like thunder on the floorboards above his head.

If he'd had to search everywhere under the hall, he never would have found the box of dynamite in time. But the burning fuse threw off sparks, and he spotted them right away in the darkness. They were almost directly under the center of the building. Logan set his jaw and dug the fingers of his right hand into the dirt to pull himself toward them.

For a second as he had looked around under the building, the thought had crossed his mind again that maybe Meadows had lied about the dynamite. He was going to feel mighty foolish if it turned out there was nothing under here. Seeing the sparks was, in a bizarre way, almost a relief. He had always liked having a goal.

This was one hell of a goal: get to that dynamite and

stop it from exploding before he and everybody still in the hall wound up blasted to kingdom come.

Logan worked his way closer and closer. His eyes had adjusted some to the gloom under the building, and the sputtering, sparking fuse gave off a little glow. He could see the wooden crate sitting on the ground. The fuse looped up and over one side of it and disappeared inside the box. As he drew closer he shoved hard with his left leg to push himself forward and stretched out his right hand as far as it would go. His fingers fell just short of the fuse's burning end. Logan cried out from the effort as he lunged for it again.

This time his hand closed around the fuse. It burned his palm, searing the skin as if he had grabbed a live coal from a fire, but he ignored that and yanked. The fuse came loose at the other end and slithered out of the box like a snake to drop onto the ground.

Darkness had enveloped Logan when his hand closed on the fuse. His grip had snuffed it out, so it was still dark under the town hall except for a little light that came down here and there through tiny cracks between the boards. He lay there breathing hard, with his face pressed against the dirt. He didn't feel the cold anymore. Didn't feel much of anything, in fact.

His hearing still worked. He heard Marshal Mahaffey yell, "Somebody crawl under there and drag him out! I want to have a word with that damned gunman, panickin' everybody and ruinin' the dance like that!"

"But Marshal," another man said, "what if there really is dynamite under there?"

"It ain't gone off, has it?" Mahaffey demanded. "Go ahead and get under there. I'd do it myself, but I'm too old."

And too stout to be crawling around under a building, Logan thought, and even after everything that had happened, a grim smile tugged at his mouth for a second.

A few moments later a hand clamped around his left ankle. A man called, "I got him! You want me to pull him out, Marshal?"

"That's what I said, wasn't it? Dadgum it, don't anybody listen to me around here?"

Whoever had crawled under the town hall to get him must have taken hold of his right leg, too, but Logan couldn't feel it. His left arm and right leg were just so much dead meat by now. But he felt himself sliding backwards along the ground, and it wasn't long before he emerged into the light of several lanterns being held up by men who had gathered around the front of the town hall.

More hands took hold of him and lifted him. His muscles wouldn't work, so the men had to catch hold of him again as soon as they let go of him. As they propped him up in front of the marshal, Mahaffey demanded, "Handley, what in the sam hill – "

"Meadows," Logan rasped. "He tried to . . . steal the bullion . . . from the Rimfire vault . . . was gonna . . . blow up the town hall . . . to cover up the robbery . . ."

"That's a lie!" a man shouted. Logan recognized him as Clete Barrows, the superintendent of the Aldena syndicate. "Meadows wouldn't do such a thing."

"You don't . . . know him like I do," Logan forced out. "He was gonna . . . double-cross you, Barrows . . . blow you up . . . along with . . . everybody else."

Barrows paled in the lanternlight, probably as he realized how close he might have come to dying.

Another man had crawled under the building. As he emerged he pushed the box of dynamite out in front of him.

"It's true, Marshal," he yelled. "Look what I found under there!"

"Son of a – " Mahaffey was so shaken he couldn't even finish the curse. He grabbed the front of Logan's vest. "Where's Meadows now?"

"I shot him . . . left him down at the Rimfire offices . . . knew I was the only one . . . who could stop the explosion . . ."

Logan broke off in a fit of coughing again, and one of the men holding him up said, "Marshal, he's burnin' up! The fever's got him bad!"

Mahaffey could be decisive when he had to. He snapped, "Somebody find Doc Johnston! Thurman, you and McClure get down to the Rimfire office right now and see if Meadows is still there. If he is, arrest him! And if he puts up a fight – " Mahaffey glanced at the box of dynamite and shuddered. "Ventilate the son of a bitch."

"Meadows is a curly wolf, Marshal. Can we take some men with us?"

"Take as many as you want. Just catch the varmint!"

Men rushed off shouting in excitement and anger. Logan let his eyes droop closed. The townspeople were safe now. The Christmas Eve dance was ruined, but at least hundreds of innocent people wouldn't have to die because of Jim Meadows' greed.

Logan started to cough again. His muscles seized up. Every wracking spasm felt like something was breaking inside him.

"Marshal, I think Handley's dyin'!" said one of the men holding him up.

Mahaffey got in Logan's face and yelled, "Blast it, don't you die, Handley! Not until I get to the bottom o' this!"

"Sorry . . . Marshal," Logan whispered. "I reckon that's . . . out of my hands now . . ."

21

The cold was gone and so were the hands holding him, along with everything else except the night's blackness. It closed in around him.

Logan didn't mind at all. He welcomed the oblivion.

3.

Logan was sixteen years old when he killed his first man. That was Kansas, 1861, a bad time and place to be. Bloody Kansas, they called it, and it more than lived up to the name. Guerrillas had swooped down on the Handley farm one night, set the barn on fire, then shot Eben Handley full of holes when he tried to defend his home and family. They had raped and murdered Logan's mother and his two younger sisters. Logan wasn't there – his father had sent him to a neighbor's farm to help them with the harvest – but he saw the orange glow in the sky and jumped on an old plow horse and rode toward home as hard as he could.

When he got there, he found two of the guerrillas coming out of the house. They were the last ones, lingering behind to do a little more looting, and when Logan galloped up and saw the barn in ruins, the huddled shape of his dead father lying on the ground, and two strangers coming drunkenly out of his house, he knew what had happened.

Before riding away from the other farm he had borrowed an old Walker Colt from the neighbor, who had carried the gun during the Mexican War. The man hadn't wanted him to take it, telling Logan that he would just get himself into trouble, but Logan had insisted.

The gun was still in his hand, and when the two raiders saw it, they tried to draw their own weapons.

Logan cocked the Walker and got off the first shot. The recoil nearly tore it out of his hand, but his aim was accurate. The heavy lead ball smashed into the chest of one guerrilla and knocked him backward into a rocking chair on the front porch.

The other man had his gun out and fired, but Logan was already off-balance from the Walker's kick and fell off the plow horse just in time to avoid being shot in the head. He landed hard in the dirt but hung on to the pistol and used both hands to steady it as he cocked it again and fired from the ground. Pure instinct guided his shot. The ball hit the second raider in the throat and angled up into his brain, dropping him like a rock.

Breathing so hard he was like a runaway steam engine, Logan climbed to his feet. He had to use both thumbs to pull the Walker's hammer back again as he stumbled toward the porch.

The second man he'd shot was dead, no doubt about that. Blood was all over the place and the ball had torn half his throat away. The first man was still wheezing, though, as he sat in the rocking chair where he had landed. The chair still moved back and forth a little, gently.

The man's gun had slipped from his fingers and lay on the porch beside the chair. His eyes were so wide they seemed like they were about to pop from their sockets. He stared at Logan and rasped, "Kid . . . I . . . I need help."

By now Logan was close enough to look through the house's open door and see the nude, crumpled body of one of his sisters lying on a throw rug that soaked up the blood from her slashed throat. Logan aimed the Walker at the surviving guerrilla's face. Even though it didn't seem possible they could, the man's eyes bulged out even more as he opened his mouth to beg for his life.

Logan pressed the trigger first, and the man's head exploded like a pumpkin dropped from a hayloft.

Before that night was over, Logan dragged the bodies of both guerrillas into the open space between the house and the burned barn. He took his father inside the house and placed both his parents in their bed after dressing his mother so she wouldn't look so indecent. He did the same for his little sisters. He took some of the money that the family had saved up and left it on the kitchen table along with a note for the neighbor explaining that the coins were payment for the horse. The note apologized, as well, for Logan not being able to return the animal. He weighted down the note with the old cap-and-ball pistol.

He gathered some supplies, a few extra clothes, and his father's rifle. He took the rifles and handguns belonging to the two guerrillas as well, along with their ammunition. He turned their mounts loose so no one could accuse him of being a horse thief.

Then he rode away and didn't look back.

It wasn't very hard to find out the names of some of the men who had been there at the farm that night. Over the next two years Logan killed nine more of them, catching each of them alone, or in one case, two at a time. By then he realized that no matter how many he killed, it wasn't going to bring his family back or ease the grief in his heart. The only thing that would do that was putting all of it behind him, once and for all.

So that was what he did. He rode away, rode west, and didn't look back. By then he had gotten pretty good at killing.

He had never really wanted to be a farmer, anyway.

Ten years had passed since then, ten long years of selling his gun to anybody who had enemies but lacked the courage or skill to deal with them himself. Logan had no idea how many men he had killed during that time. It never seemed worth the time and energy to keep a count of them.

He wasn't completely without scruples. He never backshot anybody, not once. But he had goaded men into fights when he knew they had no chance against him. Some people would claim that was the same as murder, and he didn't figure he could make much of an argument that it wasn't. He had never shot a woman or a kid, either, not even by accident.

With plenty of money most of the time, he had developed expensive tastes: good clothes, fine liquor, the occasional high-stakes game of cards, the best whores money could buy. He knew perfectly well that one of these days he would run up against somebody a hair faster on the draw and that would be the end of him, assuming somebody didn't drygulch him first or blow him apart with a shotgun blast from a dark alley some night. These things happened to a man in his line of work. He accepted that, and he slept well.

Except for the rare nights when all the dead men came back to haunt his dreams, starting with the two he had killed on the front porch of his family's home in Kansas all those years ago. They danced through his head, laughing and bleeding and dying, and all he could do was wake up in a cold sweat, gasping for breath. He shoved all that out of his mind as best he could, told himself that such dreams were just an occupational hazard, and got on with his life.

Then he had gotten a telegram from a man named John Purcell, asking him to come to a settlement in Montana Territory called Aspen Creek.

4.

October, 1874

Infantile paralysis, one of the doctors in Denver had called it, because the disease usually struck down children. Nobody knew for sure what caused it or what to do about it. Sometimes the condition seemed to get better on its own, the medico had explained to Logan. Sometimes it never did.

The Rimfire Mining Syndicate had paid for Logan to go to Denver and get medical attention. That was out of gratitude for him saving the shipment of bullion and also the lives of all those people in the town hall, although Logan had a definite feeling that the bullion was more important to the syndicate. However, that was as far as their gratitude went. A gunman who couldn't draw and fire was of no use to them.

Over time, some feeling had returned to both his left arm and his right leg. He could walk on his own now, although he had to use a cane and couldn't go very fast. His left arm was thin and withered from disuse. He could move it and could grasp things with his left hand, but the arm was too weak for him to lift much of anything with it.

The doctor in Denver had sent him to another physician in Kansas City who had more experience treating the condition. After examining Logan, that doctor had told him any recovery he made was liable to be within the first year after being stricken. Any paralysis or weakness remaining after that time was likely permanent.

Ten months had passed. Time was running out for Logan.

The doctor in Kansas City had had a suggestion, though. A town in Arkansas called Hot Springs was famous for its mineral baths that were supposed to be good for almost any ailment a person might have, including paralysis and muscle weakness.

"There's a doctor there named Strittmatter, August Strittmatter, who's supposed to have had some success treating conditions like yours," the doctor had told Logan. "His method includes a combination of muscle massage and soaking in the mineral baths. I think you should give it a try, Mr. Handley. It might be your last chance to regain more use of your limbs."

By this point, Logan was willing to try almost anything. His life was in deadly danger every day that passed with him unable to use a gun.

He had made a lot of enemies over the past dozen years, and not all of them had been left dead behind him. The ones who were still alive would like nothing better than to put a bullet in him, and if word of his affliction spread in the right circles, men would be lining up to do just that. So far he had done everything in his power to keep his condition quiet, including paying all the doctors handsomely, but sooner or later the news would get out, and if Logan couldn't defend himself by then . . .

That was why he was on a train bound for Hot Springs, gazing out the window beside him at Arkansas hillsides covered with beautiful red, orange, and gold autumn foliage.

He sat alone on one of the uncomfortable bench seats with his cane and his hat beside him. He wore no gun;

there wouldn't have been any point in it. His face was leaner than ever, his eyes set in hollow pits. Even though he knew he needed to keep his strength up, he hadn't had much of an appetite for a long time.

"Is there anything I can do for you, sir?" a woman's voice asked from the aisle.

Logan turned his head to look at her. She was reasonably attractive, around thirty years of age, well-dressed and with a wedding band on her finger. He knew she felt sorry for him because he looked like a sick man. He wasn't, really, not any more. The fever and the cough were long gone. But the damage they had done still lingered and might from now on.

He shook his head and said, "No, thank you." He knew he was being curt, but he couldn't help it. He didn't want anyone's pity, least of all that of a pretty woman. He could have played on her sympathy and gotten her to sit with him for the rest of the trip to Hot Springs, at the very least, but there was no point in it.

She frowned and said, "Are you sure? You look so tired – "

"Yes, madam, very sure," Logan said.

"All right, then." She summoned up a weak smile. "If you change your mind, I'm sitting right up – "

She stopped short again, this time because she was interrupted by the scream of the train's brakes locking down on the rails, which caused the car to lurch violently and nearly pitched the woman off her feet.

The train's abrupt slowdown threw Logan forward, too. He put his right hand on the back of the seat in front of him to brace himself.

"Oh, my Lord!" the woman exclaimed as she grasped a seat back, too, to keep herself from falling. "What's happening?"

Logan knew the train wasn't supposed to stop again before it reached Hot Springs. Also, a scheduled stop would have been much more gradual. As the car continued shuddering and slowing down, he said, "Something must be wrong. You'd better go back to your seat, ma'am."

Pale with fear, she did as he suggested. Logan stayed where he was and waited to see what was going to happen.

Whatever it was, in his condition he couldn't do much about it.

The train gave another lurch as it came to a complete stop. Logan looked out the window next to him and saw a heavily wooded slope rising only a few feet away. A glance out one of the windows on the other side of the car revealed similar terrain. The train hadn't stopped at a station somewhere, that was for sure.

This car was about half-full of passengers, and all of them were excited, upset, and a little scared. People peered out the windows and asked questions. Logan heard the words "holdup" and "robbery" more than once.

That seemed like a pretty strong possibility to Logan. He had never been a train robber, but his keen brain had no trouble figuring out how to go about stopping this train. All it would take was chopping through the trunk of a tall pine on each side of the tracks, leaving the trees still upright but ready to fall, and rigging ropes to topple them at just the right time, when the locomotive was still far enough away to stop in time but not so far back on the tracks that the engineer could stop and then reverse out of danger. One tree and the engineer might pour on the speed and try to blast through; two increased the risk of derailment too much to chance it.

Then, once the train was stopped, masked men could rush out of the forest and board the engine, take it over at gunpoint, and then spread out through the cars to rob the passengers and loot the express car. A simple plan, and Logan had a strong hunch it was being carried out at this very minute.

That hunch was confirmed a few minutes later when a man in a long duster and pulled down hat threw the door open at the front of the car and strode along the aisle with a gun in each hand. A red bandanna was tied around the lower half of his face, but what seemed to be genuine amusement sparkled in his eyes as he menaced the passengers with the weapons. A few women screamed, and several men cursed loudly and bitterly.

"No need to take on so, folks," the bandit said in a clear voice that cut through the frightened hubbub. "My friends and I don't intend to hurt anybody unless we have to. Just quiet down and we'll all get through this as fast as we can."

"I know that man," one of the male passengers said. "That's Jesse James!"

Logan suppressed the impulse to shake his head. Even if the passenger was right, announcing it like that was a pretty foolish thing to do.

But as it happened, the outlaw chuckled, evidently more amused than anything else. He said, "That's the price of fame, I suppose." Another masked, duster-clad man entered the car behind him. As the second outlaw took off his hat, Jesse James went on, "All right, folks, pony up. Wallets, watches, rings, and other valuables go into my brother's hat."

Frank James moved along the aisle to collect the loot from the passengers. One man said, "I understand you boys have a grudge against the railroads, but why take it out on the passengers? We never did anything to you or your family."

"That's true," Jesse admitted. "But you're riding on this train, and that supports the railroad. I hurt those money-grubbing scoundrels any way I can."

"It's an outrage, that's what it is," the passenger grumbled as he dropped his wallet and watch into Frank James's hat.

"Many things in life are, my friend," Jesse said.

Frank came to the woman who had offered to help Logan. She quailed back against the seat and said, "I . . . I don't have anything."

"Don't try to pull that, lady," Frank told her. "Those clothes you're wearing say different. Open up your handbag, or I'll just take the whole thing."

The woman began to sob. Frank reached for her handbag.

Logan leaned forward in his seat, without really thinking about what he was doing . . . or what he could do.

Jesse was close by in the aisle. He swung his right-hand gun toward Logan and said, "Now don't go getting any ideas, friend. Chivalry can get a man killed."

Logan looked down the barrel of the revolver and settled back against his seat. If he had still been the same man he was a year earlier, things might have been different. But . . . he wasn't.

Frank James ripped the woman's handbag away from her, opened it, and took out a coin purse. He dropped that in his hat, rummaged through the rest of the bag's contents, and then tossed it disgustedly back on the bench beside her.

Frank moved along the aisle to Logan's seat. He held out the hat and said, "Wallet in here, mister. And that better be all you reach for under your coat."

"Don't worry," Logan said. "I'm not carrying a gun."

He slid his wallet out of his pocket and dropped it in Frank's hat. Only about half of the money he had was in it; the other half was in his boot.

Frank looked hard at Logan's cane, and after a moment Logan realized the outlaw was eyeing the silver decoration on the cane's handle.

Jesse noticed, too, and said, "Forget it, Frank. I don't mind taking money from a cripple, but damned if I'm going to steal his cane."

"An outlaw with scruples," Logan said.

Jesse chuckled under the bandanna again and said, "It happens." He gestured with the right-hand gun. "Come on, Frank. Let's finish up here."

Logan sat and looked down at the toes of his boots, glad that they hadn't hadn't searched him and found the rest of his money. He hadn't had much to start with. He hadn't been able to work since being stricken with the paralysis in Aspen Creek, and months of living expenses with medical bills on top of them had eaten up most of his savings. But at least he wouldn't reach Hot Springs dead broke.

He wasn't surprised that Jesse James claimed to have scruples, either. He had read about the James brothers and their cousins the Youngers. They claimed that through their outlaw exploits they were sticking up with the common folks against the railroads and the other big businesses and the carpetbaggers from up north. That was what they liked to tell people and they probably told themselves the same thing until they came to believe it. Logan had run into hired guns who were the same way, always telling themselves that they were in the right somehow.

But the James boys and their cousins were just outlaws. Those hired guns were just killers. They could pretty it up all they wanted, but that didn't change the facts.

When Jesse and Frank had taken everybody's valuables, they moved on to the next car. This one erupted with noise again as soon as the outlaws were gone. Women wailed as their husbands tried to comfort them. Men cursed and blustered about what they would have done, if only they'd had the chance.

None of that was true, Logan thought. They had all had their chances, and they had stayed in their seats and handed over their money, just like him. They'd been scared to death.

He wasn't scared. He would have almost welcomed a bullet from Jesse James's gun. He hadn't tried anything because the sheer hopelessness of the whole thing was overwhelming. He had never minded wagering his life, but he wasn't going to throw it away.

The woman who had tried to befriend him earlier had her hands over her face as she cried. Logan put on his hat and picked up his cane. He levered himself to his feet and made his way up the aisle to her seat. As he sat down beside her, he said, "I'm sorry. I wish there was something I could have done to help."

"Oh . . . oh, no," she said. "I never would have expected . . . I mean, you couldn't . . ."

"No, I couldn't," he said. "There was a time I might have . . . but that's gone now."

A few minutes later the train's conductor burst into the car to see if everybody was all right.

"Those damned outlaws have ridden off," he reported. "We'll get moving again in a few minutes, as soon as a couple of trees are cleared off the tracks. Any able-bodied men want to volunteer to help, it'll be appreciated."

"That lets me out," Logan said quietly. For some reason he was pleased that the conductor had confirmed his speculation about how the outlaws had stopped the train.

The woman put a hand on his arm and told him, "Don't say that. It's not your fault."

"No, I suppose not," he said. He didn't really believe in a man being punished for his sins, at least not on this earth. As for what might happen beyond it, he couldn't say.

But maybe all those dead men dancing through his dreams were trying to tell him different.

5.

The town of Hot Springs lay in a winding valley that twisted between rugged, tree-covered hills. Logan had never been there before, and after growing up on the Kansas prairie and spending a lot of his time since then on the plains or in the semi-arid southwest, he found this Arkansas terrain to be beautiful. Many of the trees were pines or other evergreens, but there were trees where the leaves had turned color with the arrival of fall, so the slopes were a striking blend of different shades.

The train station buzzed with talk about the robbery, as passengers getting off told the people meeting them about being held up by the notorious James-Younger gang. No one was there to meet Logan, of course, since he didn't know anybody here, so he limped through the station lobby without anyone stopping him. The woman who had talked to him wasn't getting off the train here; she had told him that she was headed on to Little Rock, where she lived with her husband. The mildly flirtatious conversation they'd shared had taken her mind off being robbed, so Logan supposed it had done that much good, anyway.

He had only a small carpetbag, but handling it along with his cane in his one good hand made him move awkwardly through the depot. A porter offered to help him, but Logan shook his head. He had come to be stubborn about managing on his own.

"Maybe you can tell me, though, where to find Dr. August Strittmatter's clinic," he said to the man.

"Doc Strittmatter? That little foreign fella? His place is on Bathhouse Row, like all the others." The porter pointed. "Follow this street and it'll take you along the base of Hot Springs Mountain. That's where all the bathhouses are."

Logan had figured the physician would have an actual clinic, rather than just a bathhouse, but he supposed the two things could be combined. It was the hot mineral springs that were supposed to do the patients the most good, after all.

"What about a place to stay?"

The porter grinned and said, "Plenty of hotels along the row, too, sir. Just the sort for a fine gentleman like yourself."

Logan smiled. His clothes were still of good quality, but a fine gentleman needed money, too, and he had very little of that. He said, "Maybe someplace a bit more inexpensive . . ."

"Oh," the porter said in obvious understanding. "In that case, there are some boardin' houses, and most of 'em are pretty nice. Just check a couple blocks over."

Logan nodded and said, "Thanks. I'll do that."

"I can get you a buggy – "

"No, that's all right. I'll walk." He wanted to preserve as much of the money Frank and Jesse James had left him as he could.

It was a beautiful autumn day as he walked out of the station, filled with warm sunshine and a breeze that held a hint of coolness. He turned and walked a couple of blocks, as the porter had suggested, then turned again and headed along the street.

Most of the buildings appeared to be fairly new, which puzzled him at first until he decided that the town must have suffered a considerable amount of damage during the war. He hadn't really paid that much attention to the conflict after he left Kansas and headed west, but he supposed Union and Confederate forces had clashed quite a bit here in Arkansas, even if the destruction hadn't been as devastating here as it was further east in places like Georgia and Virginia.

He came to a nice-looking three-story frame house with whitewashed walls and green painted trim around the windows. A neatly printed sign that read ROOMS was propped up in one of the first floor windows. The place looked as good as any, if he could afford it, Logan thought. He turned and went along a short flagstone walk to the steps that led up to a front porch.

He had just started up those steps when the house's front door opened and a man stepped out. He saw Logan struggling to climb the steps while balancing both cane and carpetbag and said, "Here, let me give you a hand, partner."

Out of stubborn habit, Logan said, "Thanks, but I can manage by myself."

"Sure you can," the man replied, "but why should you when I'm right here?"

He came down the steps and took Logan's carpetbag. Logan tensed, ready to take a swing at the man if he tried to run off with the carpetbag.

That didn't seem to be the stranger's intention, though. He turned and fell in step beside Logan. He had a limp, too, Logan noticed as they both went up the stairs, but a much less noticeable one.

"Rusty Turner's my name," the man introduced himself. He was older than Logan, probably in his late forties judging by the touches of gray in the curly red hair that must have given him the nickname "Rusty". Barrel-chested, he wore rough work clothes and had a battered old hat shoved back on his head. He went on, "You lookin' for a place to stay?"

"That's right," Logan said.

"Well, you won't find a better place than this. Miz Eastland keeps a clean house, and she's a mighty fine cook, too. Mighty fine. You ain't lived until you've tasted her buttermilk biscuits. 'Course, it don't hurt matters that she's a mite easy on the eyes, too. Just don't get no ideas. She can be pretty stand-offish with fellas who do. Can't really blame her, I reckon, what with ever'thing she's been through. That husband o' hers, he's a dadgum fool, if you ask me."

Logan didn't recall asking Rusty Turner anything, but that didn't seem to make much difference. He could already tell that the older man liked to run his mouth. Some men were like that, although Logan had never quite been able to comprehend why. He spoke when he had something to say. He certainly wasn't in love with the sound of his own voice.

When they reached the top of the stairs and stepped onto the porch, Logan said, "I appreciate the help, Mr. Turner – "

"You ain't told me your name yet."

"It's Logan Handley." Logan didn't see what harm that would do. He had never been to Arkansas before, so he didn't expect to run into any old enemies here. Although anything was possible, he supposed. He went on, "I can take my bag now – "

"No, that's all right, I got it. Come on. Let's go inside so you can say howdy to Miz Eastland."

Arguing with Turner would be a waste of time, Logan decided, and it *was* easier to get around without having to carry his bag and handle his cane at the same time. So he just nodded and said, "Thanks," as Turner opened the door.

They went into a foyer with a nice hardwood floor covered by a woven rug. To the right was a parlor that appeared comfortably but not fancily furnished with several armchairs, a divan, and a pair of rocking chairs near a fireplace. To the left of the foyer was a dining room dominated by a long table in the center, with a couple of china cabinets along one wall. Directly ahead rose a staircase leading to the second and third floors.

A woman paused halfway down those stairs as Logan and Turner came in. The house was shadowy enough after being outside that Logan couldn't immediately make out any details about the woman except that she was tall and slender. As Rusty Turner closed the front door behind them, the woman resumed her descent.

Logan's eyes adjusted to the light enough for him to see that she was attractive, in a somewhat severe way. Her dark brown hair was pulled behind her head and gathered at the back of her neck. She wore a plain gray dress, the sort of thing he might have expected to see a widow wearing after the first few months of mourning, but Turner had referred to her as Mrs. and mentioned her husband.

"Miz Eastland, we got us a new boarder here," Turner said as the woman reached the bottom of the stairs. "This here's Mr. Handley."

"Logan Handley," Logan elaborated as he balanced himself, hooked his cane over his left arm, and reached up with his right hand to take off his hat. "It's a pleasure, Mrs. Eastland. Mr. Turner has been singing your praises ever since we encountered each other outside."

"I appreciate that," Mrs. Eastland said. "But you said Mr. Baldwin wanted to see you, Rusty, so you should go on to his office. You don't want to make him wait."

"No, I reckon not," Turner agreed. He set down Logan's carpetbag and added, "We'll be seein' you," then touched the brim of his hat, said, "Ma'am," and hurried out.

Mrs. Eastland said, "If you're looking for a room, Mr. Handley, I have one available. The cost is two dollars a week and includes breakfast and supper, as well as linens. If that's agreeable . . .?"

Logan calculated quickly in his head. He could afford to stay here for a while, but if he wanted to save up enough money to be able to afford treatments with Dr. Strittmatter, he would have to find a job. That wouldn't be easy in his condition, but he didn't see that he had any choice.

"That'll be fine," he said. He nodded toward the carpetbag. "That's all I have – "

He started to bend and reach for the bag's handle. The woman leaned forward at the same time, and he realized she must have thought he was asking for her help. He said, "I've got it," and the words came out sharper than he intended.

She straightened and said, "All right." Her tone was cool, and Logan remembered what Rusty Turner had said about her being stand-offish if a fellow got the wrong idea about her. Logan didn't have any ideas about her, right or wrong, but it appeared that he rubbed her the wrong way regardless.

That was all right. He hadn't come to Hot Springs looking for friends.

"I'd like a week's rent in advance," she went on.

Logan frowned as he remembered that all the money he had in the world was cached in his boot. He couldn't very well sit down right here on the foyer and take it off, so he said, "If I could pay you later today . . ."

"All right. Before supper."

"Yes, of course," he agreed.

"I'll show you the room," she said as she turned toward the stairs. Then she paused and looked over her shoulder at him. "Are you able to climb stairs, Mr. Handley?"

"Yes, ma'am, as long as I don't have to rush too much."

"Take your time," she told him. "The room isn't going anywhere."

He was almost out of breath by the time he reached the second floor landing, but he made an effort not to let her know that. He didn't ask for sympathy from anyone and preferred not to have it offered.

The room was two doors down from the landing, and not surprisingly, based on what he had seen in the rest of the house, it was very clean and well-kept. A bed, a wardrobe, a dressing table with a basin and chair, a single window with a light blue curtain decorated with yellow flowers . . . All the comforts of home, Logan told himself, and the thought was tinged with bitterness because a home was one thing he hadn't had for many years.

"This will do me just fine," he told her. He set the carpetbag on the bed.

"Supper is at six o'clock. The linens were just changed."

"Thank you." As she started to turn away, Logan added, "Ah, Mrs. Eastland . . . you wouldn't happen to know of anyone around here who's looking to hire some help, do you?"

"What is it you do, Mr. Handley?"

Well, I used to kill other men like me . . .

He couldn't very well say that, so he said, "Whatever I can turn my hand to these days. I need a job, so I can't exactly be choosy."

"Talk to Rusty when he comes back." For the first time, he heard a bit of warmth in the woman's voice as she added, "He knows just about everyone in Hot Springs."

Logan could believe that. Rusty Turner had seemed the sort to make friends immediately.

Mrs. Eastwood left the room. Logan tossed his hat on the bed next to the carpetbag and sat down, relieved to be able to get off his feet. The walk from the train station was the longest he had made in quite a while. Maybe having to get around in this hilly town would help him to build up his strength. Either that, or finish the job of doing him in.

Not for the first time, he thought that he would have been better off if the disease that had stricken him had killed him rather than crippling him. Death might have been easier to accept than living like this, with no real hopes and facing only a struggle for survival until his past caught up to him.

Maybe seeing Dr. Strittmatter would change things. Maybe the doctor could at least offer him the possibility of improvement.

Or if he was able to get a job and earn some money, he might buy a gun to replace the ones he had sold after getting sick.

He was sure he'd be able to find a use for it.

6.

When Logan came down a little early for supper, he found Mrs. Eastland setting a bowl of potatoes on the table in the dining room. None of the other boarders were in the dining room, but he heard what sounded like several people talking in the parlor.

He held out a ten dollar gold piece to her and said, "I wanted to give you this."

She took it, said, "Thank you," and dropped it in the pocket of the apron she was wearing. "Are you just paying for one week? Would you like change back?"

Logan shook his head.

"No, that'll cover my room and board for more than a month. I'm expecting to be here for that long."

"Very well. Supper isn't quite ready, but you can wait in the parlor with the others."

Clearly, she didn't want to chat with him, but he could understand that. She still had work to do. He smiled for a second, nodded, and walked across the foyer to the parlor.

Rusty Turner was sitting in one of the armchairs, smoking a pipe. He took it out of his mouth and poked the stem at another man, evidently to emphasize a point in whatever story he was telling at the moment. The other man laughed.

Logan's gaze flicked around the room. It was his custom to size up the inhabitants any time he entered a room, and he hadn't bothered trying to break that habit.

There were seven people in this one, including Rusty. The other half-dozen were equally divided between men and women. Two of the women were white-haired and elderly; the other was in late middle age, not far from there. The man Rusty was talking to was about the same age as him, late forties or early fifties. The other two were somewhat younger and had the look of clerks about them.

They weren't a very impressive bunch, but they appeared to be a lot more stable and law-abiding than the backshooters, tinhorn gamblers, and whores among whom Logan had spent so many years, not particularly enjoying their company but figuring that was where he belonged.

"There he is now," Rusty said as Logan came into the room. He stood up, waved the hand holding the pipe at Logan, and went on, "This is the new boarder I was tellin' you about, Logan Handley. Come on in and meet all the folks, Logan."

Everybody was on an informal basis with Rusty, Logan realized. He nodded pleasantly enough and managed to smile as Rusty led him around the room performing introductions, but the names of the other boarders vanished from Logan's mind almost as soon as he heard them. He wasn't accustomed to having to remember such things. To him, no one except his enemies and his allies had mattered for a long time.

But now, like it or not, he was a common man, so he would have to make an effort to be more civil. None of the other boarders made any comment about his obvious affliction, and Logan appreciated that.

"What's your line of work, Mr. Handley?" one of the clerks asked. His name was Claude Something-or-other, Logan recalled.

"Right now that's a good question," he said. "In fact, I'm looking for a job. Mrs. Eastland suggested that I ask you about that, Mr. Turner."

"Did she now?"

"Yes, she said you know practically everyone in Hot Springs."

Rusty slapped his thigh and laughed. He said, "Vickie's right about that, she is. And I have something in mind that might suit you just fine, Logan. I'll tell you about it later."

Logan wasn't sure why Rusty didn't just go ahead and tell him about it now, but he nodded and said, "All right."

A few minutes later, Mrs. Eastland – Vickie, Rusty had called her – came in and announced that supper was ready. Everyone trooped into the dining room to eat.

Rusty hadn't been exaggerating about the quality of Vickie Eastland's cooking. Logan had eaten in some of the finest restaurants in the country and in the dining room of the best hotels, and the food in this Hot Springs boarding house was easily their equal. The fare was simple enough – roast beef, ham, potatoes, greens, corn on the cob, gravy, and those buttermilk biscuits Rusty had mentioned – but everything tasted delicious. For months now Logan hadn't had much of an appetite and usually found himself picking at his food wherever he ate, but tonight, surrounded by the pleasant conversation at the table, he ate as heartily as he had in a long time.

If nothing else, he thought, Vickie Eastland's cooking might strengthen him up a mite.

One thing he noticed was that Mrs. Eastland's mysterious husband didn't put in an appearance. Rusty had called the man a fool, Logan remembered, and to miss a meal like this he would have to be.

After supper, most of the boarders went back to the parlor, but Rusty caught Logan's eye and said, "There are rockers out on the front porch. Let's sit out there and enjoy the evening air, shall we?"

"All right," Logan said. Maybe Rusty would tell him about that job. Logan intended to find Dr. Strittmatter's place the next day and talk to the physician so he could find out how much money he would need to begin treatment, so it would help if he had an idea of how much he might be able to make.

Logan's cane thumped on the porch boards as they went outside. Rusty waved him into one of the rocking chairs and took the chair next to the one where Logan settled back. He took out his pipe and a tobacco pouch and started packing tobacco into the bowl again.

When he had scraped a match alight and puffed the pipe to life, he said, "Vickie don't really care for smokin' in the house, but she don't fuss about this pipe o' mine too much, bless her heart. It's cigars she won't abide. Carleton smoked cigars."

"Carleton?" Logan repeated.

"Carleton Eastwood. Used to be Vickie's husband."

"He's dead?" That would explain why he hadn't shown up for dinner, Logan thought.

But Rusty made a disgusted sound and said, "Not hardly. He divorced her."

That was surprising. Divorce wasn't unheard of, but it was rare and when it happened, it was usually accompanied by scandal of some sort. Vickie Eastwood struck Logan as being far too cool and stiff-necked for scandal.

He gave in to curiosity and asked, "What happened?"

"I'm a talker, not a gossiper," Rusty replied with a shake of his head. "So I'll leave it at that except to say that Miz Eastwood is a decent woman and I don't believe a word of what was said about her."

Considering all the disreputable things Logan had done in his life, he wasn't just about to look down in judgment on Vickie Eastwood, no matter what she was accused of doing.

"Now you've made me more interested than ever," he said. "I won't press you, though. At least not about that. I *am* curious about that job you mentioned, though."

"I've got a friend named Doc Reese – "

"A doctor?" Logan leaned forward in the rocking chair. He didn't know what sort of job he could get with a doctor, but the idea intrigued him.

Rusty took care of that thought by saying, "No, he's a barber. Folks just call him Doc because, well, you know, barbers have always done some doctorin', too."

With a grunt, Logan sat back. He was well aware that in many frontier communities, the local barber was the closest thing to a sawbones the settlers had. But that usually meant setting broken bones, dosing ailments with dubious tonics, and maybe patching up bullet holes. The chances of a barber being able to help him with his condition were non-existent, he thought.

Rusty went on, "Doc's lookin' for somebody to help him out at the shop. You know, sweepin' out and such like. I don't reckon the pay would be much, but I thought he might be able to give you a hand with whatever it is that ails you, too."

"Everybody's been so careful not to mention my condition, I was beginning to think you were all blind."

"Not hardly. I reckon you saw I've got a bit of a limp myself." Rusty slapped his right thigh again. "Know how I got it?"

"I don't have any idea," Logan said.

"A Yankee bullet when we were fightin' 'em in the Wilderness. Tore up the muscles so bad one of those field hospital butchers they called a doctor wanted to hack it off. He would have, too, if I hadn't put a gun to his head and told him to sew it up instead. I didn't lose the leg, but by the time I got home it was so weak I could barely use it."

Logan was interested in the story despite his disappointment at Doc Reese turning out to be a barber. He said, "That's a little different. My problems weren't caused by bullet wounds. I had an illness. Something called infantile paralysis, because it usually strikes young children."

Logan wasn't sure why he had told Rusty that much. He hadn't really discussed his condition with anyone other than the doctors he had gone to, let alone spilling the story to an almost stranger. Rusty Turner possessed a quality Logan had seen in other men, however, an ability to put people at ease and get them talking to him. Maybe it was because he was such a big talker himself.

Rusty puffed on the pipe for a moment and then waved the hand holding it as if to dismiss what Logan had just said.

"If muscles are weak and don't work, I don't know that the cause really matters. What you've got to do is get 'em strong again, and that's what Doc helped me do. I don't reckon my leg will ever be completely back to normal, but it almost is and that's good enough for me. You should at least talk to him, Logan."

"About the job, you mean."

Rusty shrugged and said, "Sure, about the job. And anything else you want to."

Logan figured that the wages for sweeping out a barber shop would be pitiful. It might take him years of working there to save up enough for him to afford Dr. Strittmatter's help. Years that he didn't have.

But it was a start, and it might pay enough to keep him in bed and board while he looked for something better. This wasn't like the old days, when men sought him out and offered him large sums of money to work for them.

Of course, if he was working in a barber shop, he probably wouldn't have to shoot anybody, either, he reminded himself.

"Where do I find this Doc Reese's place?" he asked.

"I'll take you there first thing in the morning," Rusty promised. "I've got to make a run, but it'll be later before everything's loaded and ready to go."

"A run?"

"I drive a freight wagon for Mr. Marcus Baldwin," Rusty explained. "Nobody in Arkansas handles a team of jugheaded mules better'n ol' Rusty Turner, let me tell you."

"All right. I appreciate the help."

"Us gimpy-legged fellas got to stick together. If you don't mind me askin', what was it you did before you was afflicted with this . . . infantile paralysis, you said? You strike me as bein' a real gentleman. A gambler, maybe?"

"You could call it that," Logan said, but he didn't offer a more detailed explanation.

In truth, that was a pretty good description, though.

He had gambled with men's lives . . . including his own.

7.

If anything, breakfast the next morning was better than supper the night before. Logan could have lingered over another cup of Vickie Eastland's excellent coffee, but Rusty only had so much time before he had to leave on that freight run and Logan wanted the introduction to Doc Reese. So the two men walked out of the boarding house – both limping, one just more pronounced than the other – and headed for Hot Springs' business district.

Logan spotted the red, white, and blue striped barber pole before they reached the shop, which sat in a small brick building between a shoemaker's shop and an apothecary. Directly across the street was Dumont's Saloon. That was handy, Logan thought. If he got the job, he might need a drink by the time he had spent all day sweeping up clippings in the barber shop.

Logan wore the trousers from his suit today, but at Rusty's suggestion he had left off the coat, vest, and string tie.

"Go in there dressed like a swell, and Doc might be less likely to offer you the job," Rusty had said. "Not that Doc's stuck-up in any way. But you might have better luck if you look more like a workin' man."

"That's what I am now, I suppose," Logan had said. "At least that's what I'm trying to be."

It was early in the day, but when they went into the shop, Doc Reese already had a customer in hic chair and another man waiting for a haircut. Rusty hailed him cheerfully, saying, "Good mornin', Doc!"

Reese was a short, stocky man with blond hair and a neatly trimmed mustache. He wore gray striped trousers, a darker gray vest, white shirt, and black tie. As he clipped the hair of the man who sat in the chair with a white cloth draped over his chest and lap, Reese said, "Hello, Rusty. Who's your friend?"

"This here is Logan Handley. He's a new boarder at Miz Eastland's house."

"Hello, Mr. Handley," Reese said. He seemed friendly enough, if a little reserved with strangers. "Come to get a haircut?"

"Actually, I could probably use one," Logan said with a smile. "It's been a while, and I'm getting a little shaggy." He crooked his left arm, hung the cane over it, and took off his hat. He hung it on the hat rack just inside the shop's entrance and went on, "It's a pleasure to meet you, Mr. Reese."

"Call me Doc. Everybody does."

"All right, Doc."

"Actually," Rusty said, "Logan here is lookin' for a job. You haven't hired anybody yet to help out around here, have you, Doc?"

"As a matter of fact, no." Reese paused in his hair-cutting and frowned slightly. "But I figured I'd probably hire a kid, or maybe an old-timer who's not looking to make a living . . ."

"I could sure use the work, Doc," Logan said. The words threatened to stick in his throat, and he had to force them out. It was a bitter thing, having to beg for a job like this, but his future, if he was going to have one, depended on it.

Rusty said, "And there's more to it than that. Logan's

had some problems, as you can see, and I was hopin' maybe you could help him the way you helped me after I was hurt."

Doc nodded toward a couple of empty chairs and said, "Why don't the two of you sit down? We'll talk about it in a little while, after I finish with these fellas."

"I've got to head on over to Mr. Baldwin's wagon yard," Rusty said, "but Logan doesn't have to be anywhere, do you, Logan?"

"No. I don't have anywhere I have to be."

It bothered him to admit that, too, but there was no denying the facts.

"Can you find your way back to the boardin' house?" Rusty asked.

"Yes, I think so." Logan had tracked men through rugged mountains and across vast prairies and blazing deserts. He thought he could manage a few blocks of Hot Springs.

"I'll see you later, then." With a casual wave, Rusty left the barber shop.

Logan sat there and looked around while the scissors in Doc Reese's hand *snick-snicked* around the customer's head.

The shop had only the one barber chair that swiveled on its base and had a leather-covered rest for the customer's feet. An array of colorful bottles containing hair tonic sat on the polished wooden counter along the right-hand wall, and a large mirror covered the wall above the counter. Several straight-backed chairs where customers could wait their turn were placed along the other wall, which was decorated with signs advertising hair tonics, shampoos, and restorers. A painting depicting an English hunting scene, complete with foxhounds and galloping horses, hung on the rear wall. It was a comfortable place, although Logan wasn't sure he would want to spend all his days here.

He could stand it for a while, though, until he found something better. At least as long as he worked here, he probably wouldn't have to worry about being kicked out of the boarding house.

Doc Reese wasn't as talkative as some barbers Logan had seen, although he chatted pleasantly enough with his customers. He finished up with the first man, who paid and went on his way. The second man was balding, so it didn't take as long to cut his hair. When he was gone, Doc said to Logan, "If you'd like, you can grab that broom in the corner and sweep up these clippings. I've been doing it myself, but when things get really busy I don't have time. Decided I'd rather have somebody around to take care of it, as well as for company during the slack times."

"Sure," Logan said as he got to his feet. He limped over to the broom, leaned his cane against the wall, and used the broom to help keep his balance instead as he began to sweep. For a moment, the humiliation of his situation soured his stomach, but he began to get over that as he concentrated on doing a good job.

He had always prided himself on being a professional, after all.

Doc sat down in the barber chair and said, "You were ill, weren't you?"

"Infantile paralysis, one of my doctors called it," Logan answered without looking up from what he was doing.

"I thought that might be it. I've seen cases of it before, you know. People come here to Hot Springs thinking the mineral baths will cure it."

"Aren't the baths supposed to help things like that?" Logan asked. This time he paused in his sweeping and looked up at Doc.

The barber shrugged and said, "If you ask some people, the baths are good for whatever ails you. Anything and everything. I'm not so sure, though. You've got one bad arm and one bad leg?"

"Left arm, right leg."

"Not an apoplectic seizure, then," Doc said. "Those usually confine their damage to one side of the body. I'd agree with the doctor who told you your condition is due to an attack of infantile paralysis. Those muscles hurt, don't they?"

"Sometimes a great deal."

"The mineral baths will help with the pain, no doubt about that."

"What about the weakness?" Logan asked.

Doc shook his head and said, "Nothing but using them – making them hurt even more – will do anything for that."

"Dr. August Strittmatter claims that the mineral baths will restore strength and function to damaged muscles."

Doc made a face.

"Dr. Strittmatter," he repeated. "I've heard all about his claims."

"You don't believe them?"

"I don't like to criticize a man when I've never even met him . . . but I just don't see how what he says can be right."

Logan realized he was leaning on the broom rather than sweeping and thought that might not be a good thing for him to do when Doc Reese hadn't actually offered him a job yet. He started sweeping again, but he said, "Rusty told me that you helped him when he came back from the war. He barely limps now."

"It took a lot of time and effort on his part. I don't really deserve much credit. Rusty did all the real work."

"Still, he thought you might be able to help me."

Doc frowned in thought for a long moment, then finally nodded.

"I suppose I could give it a try, especially if you're going to be working here. You want the job?"

Logan hesitated. If he did this, his life was going to be a lot different than it had ever been before.

Of course, it was already completely different from the existence he had led before that Christmas Eve night in Montana Territory. He said, "Yes, Doc, I do. When do I start?"

Doc chuckled and said, "Looks to me like you already have."

* * *

Doc stayed fairly busy all day, and so did Logan. When he wasn't sweeping, there were other odd jobs around the shop that he could do, such as taking the smaller bottles of hair tonic into the storage room in the back and refilling them. Doc bought the stuff by the gallon jug. As it turned out, Logan was on his feet most of the day, and by the time Doc turned the CLOSED sign around in the window late that afternoon, the muscles in Logan's right leg throbbed from the unaccustomed use.

He sat down to rub the leg while Doc folded the cape and laid it over the back of the chair.

"Leg muscles hurting, are they?" he asked.

Logan nodded without looking up and said, "Yeah, some."

"That's good, you know. Shows that you used them more today than you're used to. Just be ready for the fact that they'll be even sorer tomorrow morning."

"I expect you're right."

"Still want the job?"

Logan looked up and nodded. "Yeah, I do."

"Want me to pay you for what you did today?"

Logan considered that, then shook his head. He said, "No, wait until I've earned more. I'm paid up at the boarding house for a few weeks, so I don't really need any more right now."

He had forgotten all about thinking that he might stop at Dumont's Saloon for a drink when the day's work was over. He was more concerned with getting back to the boarding house by the time everyone sat down to supper. He didn't want to come in late to one of Vickie Eastland's meals.

"All right. I reckon I'll see you tomorrow."

Logan pushed himself to his feet and said, "You sure will." He took his cane and left the barber shop.

He walked at his usual slow pace toward the boarding house. His route took him along Bathhouse Row, and this time he noticed a large white building with columns out front. One of those columns had a brass plaque on it, and when Logan came closer he was able to make out the writing on the plaque. It read STRITTMATTER MINERAL BATHS. In smaller letters underneath those words was the name DR. AUGUST STRITTMATTER.

The bathhouse was open. A few well-dressed men and women were going in and out. Logan paused to watch them for a moment, and while he was doing that, a buggy pulled up and stopped in front of the building. Logan glanced toward the vehicle and saw a short, rotund man in a dark suit and hat climbing out. He was clean-shaven, and in fact Logan didn't see any hair underneath the man's hat, either. He seemed to be bald as an egg. The man looked at Logan through round, rimless spectacles and nodded pleasantly.

"Good evening, *mein herr*," the man said.

"*Guten abend*," Logan replied.

The stranger looked surprised. He said, "You speak *Deutsche*?"

"A little." Logan smiled. "*Ein bisschen*."

He didn't explain that he spoke the little German he did because he had once spent most of a long, snowy winter in a Dakota Territory settlement with a Prussian whore named Ilsa. To pass the time, she had taught him some of the language.

The bald little man rattled off something that Logan didn't understand except a word here and there. Still smiling, he shook his head and said, "Sorry, but I'm afraid you lost me on most of that."

"I was asking about your injury." The man motioned toward the cane.

"It's not actually from an injury. I got sick. The doctors say the illness damaged some of my nerves."

"Ah. The paralysis. Yes, I am quite familiar with such conditions. I am a physician myself. Dr. August Strittmatter."

The possibility that this man might be Dr. Strittmatter had occurred to Logan, but he didn't really expect it to turn out to be true. And yet it made sense, because this bathhouse did belong to the doctor.

"I'm Logan Handley," Logan introduced himself.

"Are you considering taking the baths?" Strittmatter nodded toward the impressive building in front of them. "They would do you much good, my young friend."

"I would, but . . . I can't afford it right now."

"*Ach*, well, too bad." Strittmatter patted Logan's upper arm. "You come see me when you can. We will make a new man out of you, you will see."

He didn't really want to be a new man, Logan thought as he watched Strittmatter waddle into the bathhouse.

He just wanted the old one back.

Or did he? During the years he had packed a gun, he had never allowed himself to think too much about what he was doing for a living. The past months of forced inactivity had allowed time for doubts to creep into his mind. If his muscles ever returned to normal, did he want to pick up a gun again? Did he want to face a man, knowing that in another few moments one of them would likely be dead?

Or would his nerves break if he even tried?

With no answers to those questions, Logan turned away from the big building and walked toward the boarding house.

8.

Doc Reese was certainly right about Logan's muscles being sore the next morning. He groaned as he pulled himself out of bed. His left leg didn't want to move, and it tried to buckle when he put weight on it. Stubbornly, he stiffened it and willed it to not only hold him up but to help carry him across the room and downstairs as well.

He didn't let Vickie Eastland or any of the other boarders see that he was hurting. He didn't want their sympathy. Rusty wasn't back from his freight run, so Logan didn't have to hide anything from him.

The second day at the barber shop was much the same as the first, and so were the third and the fourth . . . and almost before Logan knew it, a week had passed. Rusty was back in Hot Springs, and he was the only one who knew how much pain Logan really was in. It was too difficult to keep that from Rusty, who turned out to be an astute observer of the human condition.

Also after a week's time, Doc paid Logan's wages, dropping several coins into his palm. Logan had never been paid so little for a job in all his life, but he felt a surprising touch of pride as he closed his hand around the money.

Late that afternoon when Doc closed for the day and Logan left the barber shop, he glanced across the street at Dumont's and thought that maybe one beer wouldn't hurt. Just to celebrate completing his first week of working at a real job. He limped across the street and went into the saloon.

Unlike some of the saloons in Hot Springs, Dumont's didn't cater to the wealthy visitors who came to town for the mineral baths. Like Doc's barber shop, the customers here were more working class folks, although the place was fairly clean and neatly kept for a saloon. The hour was fairly early for the saloon trade, so the room wasn't crowded. About half of the tables were occupied, and there was plenty of open space at the bar. That was where Logan headed.

He hooked his cane on the edge of the bar, rested both hands on the hardwood, and carefully propped his right foot on the brass rail to ease the muscles in his bad leg. A bartender in a white shirt, red vest, black bow tie, and sleeve garters came over to him. The man sported a handlebar mustache and his brown hair was parted in the center. Logan smiled and had to swallow a laugh because the man looked like a caricature of a bartender in a cheap melodrama. The mustache appeared to be real, though, not fake.

"What can I get for you, friend?" the man asked.

"Beer," Logan said. "If it's cold."

"Coldest this side of St. Louis," the bartender claimed. Logan doubted if the claim was true, but as long as the beer wasn't warm, he didn't really care.

He slid four bits across the bar as the man placed a mug in front of him. The beer was definitely cool and tasted good going down.

The bartender lingered on the other side of the hardwood and said, "Seen you before."

"Have you?" Logan said.

"Yep. Comin' out of Doc Reese's shop every day. You workin' over there? You a barber?"

Logan shook his head. "No, I'm just giving Doc a hand."

"Wish somebody would give me one," the man muttered.

Logan glanced around and said, "No offense, but you don't look all that busy."

"Not right now. Wait a couple of hours. From then until midnight I'll be runnin' up and down this bar so much my tongue'll be hangin' out." The bartender extended his right hand. "Name's Dewey, by the way. Dewey Dumont. My folks had kind of a questionable sense of humor."

Logan instinctively liked the man. He shook hands with Dumont, and as he did, an idea occurred to him.

"You sound like a man who could use some help, Mr. Dumont. I assume you own this place?"

"Indeed I do, sir. And I've fired half a dozen bartenders in the past year. Can't seem to find a man who's really willlin' to work."

"You've found one now," Logan said. He told Dumont his name.

"Are you askin' for a job?"

"I am if you're offering one," Logan said. He was already pushing his body beyond the limits of what it was accustomed to, so this might not be a very good idea, but at the same time he had to ask himself if he could be that much more tired and sore than he already was. The answer was probably yes, he mused, but the extra money would put him that much closer to being able to afford treatments from Dr. Strittmatter.

Dumont rubbed his chin and frowned. He said, "Let me think on that, Mr. Handley. I couldn't help but notice that you ain't real spry when it comes to gettin' around."

"That's true, but I'm getting better," Logan lied. "My leg is getting stronger."

"Do you mean to give up workin' in the barber shop to tend bar? And for that matter, have you ever tended bar before?"

"To answer your last question first . . . no, not really, but I've been on the other side of the bar plenty of times. And you said you're only really busy in the evenings, so I thought that's when I'd work. I can keep on working for Doc at the same time. He closes early enough for me to get to my boarding house, have supper, and then come back here to give you a hand."

"It ain't as easy as it looks, you know," Dumont said. "Bartendin', I mean."

"I'm sure it's not. But I pick up on things quickly."

You wouldn't believe how quickly I learned how to kill, Logan thought.

"I suppose it couldn't hurt anything to give it a try," Dumont said with a shrug. "I warn you, though, I'm a stern taskmaster."

"And I'm a hard worker. That means we should get along just fine."

Dumont laughed and said, "You're not lackin' for confidence, friend, I'll give you credit for that much." He hadn't picked up the coins that Logan put down to pay for his beer. Now he pushed them back across the bar and went on, "I'll give those back to you as well, but that's the last beer you'll get on the house, at least while you're working."

"I'm not working now."

"Close enough. Can you start tonight?"

Logan picked up the mug, drank the rest of the beer in it, and said, "I'll be back."

* * *

Logan just thought he was tired before. By the time the evening rush was over at Dumont's and Dewey told him he could go home, the sort of bone-deep weariness that Logan hadn't experienced in years had seeped into his body. The walk back to the boarding house was only a few blocks, but it seemed like a hundred miles to him. And the stairs leading up to the second floor were as steep as the Grand Tetons . . .

But as the days passed, he found that like Doc Reese, Dewey Dumont was a good man to work for, and not nearly as hard-nosed an employer as he had made himself out to be. As a matter of fact, Dewey was something of a soft touch, and his customers knew it. When they were running low on funds, he would let them have a drink on the cuff, as long as they didn't try to abuse his generosity.

Logan's life as a feared gunman receded farther into his memory. Back then he had spent his days and nights enjoying the finest food, drink, lodging, and female company that money could buy, when he wasn't actually working. Now he was surrounded by people he would have considered common, in the boarding house and at both of his jobs. He was finding that he liked them, too, and was glad to be around them.

The work was hard, though, and as far as he could tell it hadn't strengthened his muscles. He still limped heavily, and his left arm was too weak for him to do much with it. When he tried, he wound up with it aching all the way up into his shoulder and neck.

The arm hurt particularly bad one night after he had worked at the saloon for a couple of weeks. By the time he got back to the boarding house, the place was dark except for a lamp turned low in the parlor. He knew that Vickie Eastland didn't like her boarders coming in late like this; when he had told her about the job at the saloon, her mouth had pursed in disapproval for a second before she controlled the reaction.

"I won't ask that you don't take the job, Mr. Handley," she had said. "I wouldn't interfere with any man's employment. But I will ask that you be as quiet as possible when you come in at night, to avoid disturbing any of the other residents."

"Of course," Logan had promised.

He had lived up to that, being careful not to thump his cane too loudly on the floor when he was moving around. He was in the habit, too, of going into the parlor to blow out the lamp Vickie left burning for him. That way she didn't have to worry about it.

Tonight when he went into the parlor to do that, his tiredness caught up to him and he sank down in one of the armchairs, figuring that he would sit there for a few minutes and catch his breath before he blew out the lamp and went upstairs.

Without thinking about what he was doing, he reached across his body with his right hand and began to massage his aching left shoulder. He rested his head against the back of the chair and closed his eyes.

He had been sitting there like that for several minutes when he suddenly felt a light touch from behind him. Vickie Eastland said, "Let me do that for you."

Logan turned his head and looked back in surprise. She stood behind the chair. Her hair was loose for a change, and she wore a dressing gown tightly belted around the waist and closed up to her throat. Still, this was certainly the most informal he had seen her since he had been living in her house.

"I'd like that," he told her. He turned his head around to the front and closed his eyes again as her fingers began to dig into his shoulder with surprising firmness. At the same time, her touch had a soothing gentleness about it. The combination worked its way into his sore, tight muscles and made them loosen in relief.

After a moment Logan wanted to groan in pleasure, but instead he kept his eyes closed and said, "You do that . . . very well."

"I used to rub my husband's shoulders like this," Vickie said. Then, as if she just realized what she had said, she drew in a sharp breath.

Logan didn't know what to say. He still had no idea what had caused the two of them of them to divorce, and he wasn't going to pry into something that was none of his business.

Instead he said awkwardly, "I'm sure he found it quite enjoyable."

Vickie took her hands away, much to Logan's regret. She said, "I didn't mean anything by that comment, Mr. Handley. I certainly did not mean to . . . to compare you to anyone else, including my former husband."

"I know that, Mrs. Eastland. You're just kind-hearted. You can't stand to see anyone suffering . . . even a man."

He wasn't sure what prompted him to say that. The words came out harsher than he intended. Harsh enough to make Vickie take a step back. When he looked around at her, her face was set in hard lines.

"I'll say good night now," she said coldly. "Please be as quiet as possible when you're going upstairs."

"Of course," Logan said. He wished the moment of friendliness between them hadn't gotten shattered so easily. Obviously, whatever feelings she had been experiencing were fragile ones. He hadn't meant to hurt her.

He sat there a few more minutes then blew out the lamp and went upstairs, being careful not to thump his cane on the stairs.

9.

The brief thaw on Vickie's part was only temporary; Logan's thoughtless words had seen to that. She wasn't unfriendly, necessarily, but over the next few weeks she was as cool as ever, mirroring the weather advancing through the autumn toward winter.

Logan spent very little money. He took his lunches at a hash house not far from the barber shop, where he could get a decent meal for ten cents. Dewey Dumont treated him to an occasional beer when he wasn't working. The two dollars a week he paid to Vickie for room and board represented his biggest expense.

Because of that, the wages he earned from Doc and Dewey began to add up, and it occurred to Logan that the smart thing to do would be to put the money in the bank, instead of stashing it in the wardrobe in his room at the boarding house, as he had been doing.

On a cool, blustery day in November, he decided to skip lunch and use the time to pay a visit to the bank instead. He took the money he had saved with him, carrying the coins in a leather pouch he stuck in his coat's inner pocket. They made a nice, satisfying lump.

The bank was down the hill from the bathhouses, an appropriately solid-looking red brick edifice. When Logan went inside at midday, he found himself in the usual hushed atmosphere of a financial institution. It was odd, he thought, how banks and churches had some of the same sort of feel about them, an aura that made people lower their voices and walk softly. That was because some people worshipped money, he supposed. He had been guilty of that himself, at least to a certain extent.

During the years he had spent as a well-paid gunman, he'd had bank accounts in both Denver and San Francisco. His medical expenses had cleaned them out. Today was the first time he had set foot in a bank for months.

Several desks were arranged in two rows behind a low, gated railing to his left. Stuffy-looking men in suits sat at those desks. Behind them was a door that probably led to the bank president's private office. A line of tellers' cages was in front of Logan, with a high counter to the right where customers could make out deposit or withdrawal forms and write in their bank books. It was empty at the moment. Two of the tellers had customers, but the third man wasn't busy, and as Logan approached, he said, "May I help you, sir?"

Logan stepped up to the cage, took the pouch from his pocket, and set it on the counter.

"I'd like to open an account and deposit this, please."

"Of course, sir." The teller picked up a pencil and a piece of paper to take down Logan's particulars.

Before he could write anything, he glanced over Logan's shoulders, and the way the teller's eyes suddenly got wide and scared told Logan something was wrong. He looked behind him and saw five men barging into the bank. Each man wore a duster, a pulled-down hat, and a bandanna tied over the lower half of his face. They all brandished guns.

Instantly, Logan's brain flashed back to the train robbery and his encounter with Frank and Jesse James. His first thought was that the James boys had come to Hot Springs to hold up the bank.

But then the man in the lead yelled through his mask, "Nobody move! Everybody stick your hands in the air or we'll start shootin'!"

The robber's voice had a ragged, nervous quality that was a far cry from the cool, measured tones of Jesse James. These men weren't veteran desperadoes like the James-Younger gang. They were all jittery as they spread out across the lobby and menaced the customers and bank employees with their revolvers.

Amateurs, Logan thought scornfully. They were scared. It was entirely possible this was the first bank they had ever held up.

But a nervous man with a gun was a dangerous thing. Logan turned slowly away from the counter and held up both hands in plain sight. The left one trembled from the effort it took to use his weakened arm.

"That's right," the leader of the outlaws said, his words still slightly muffled by the bandanna. "Just do like we say, or we'll kill everybody in here."

Outlandish threats like that were another sign of inexperience. Gunshots would draw a lot of attention. The outlaws wouldn't want that.

In a way, this hold-up probably *was* Jesse James's fault, Logan thought. Jesse's fame had spread across the whole country and inspired a lot of would-be desperadoes. Jesse had made daring daylight robberies like this glamorous. Logan had run into plenty of young gunmen who wanted nothing more than to be famous, even if it cost them their lives doing it.

Logan and the other two customers were herded at gunpoint over to the side counter, where one robber covered them while two others got the tellers to come out of their cages and join the customers. Meanwhile one of the other outlaws covered the clerks while the leader went to the door of the bank president's office and banged on it with his fist.

"Come on outta there!" the leader shouted. "We'll start shootin' folks if you don't!"

The door opened tentatively. The boss outlaw reached in with his free hand, grabbed the bank president by the front of his vest and shirt, and hauled him out. A hard shove sent the man sprawling on top of one of the desks. That upset an inkwell and caused a black pool of ink to spread over the blotter.

"You're gonna open up the vault now," the outlaw ordered. "Get to it."

The bank president summoned up a little bit of courage and said, "If you kill me, you'll never get the vault open."

"Oh, I won't kill you," the outlaw said, and Logan could almost see the sneer on his face through the bandanna. "I'll just blow one of your knees apart." He eared back the hammer on his gun and pointed it at the bank president's leg. "You want that, mister? You want pain and misery for the rest of your life?"

Those words kindled a fire of anger inside Logan. He knew what it was like to be crippled, although his condition wasn't the result of a gunshot wound, and he didn't like to hear anyone else being threatened with that. But with an outlaw's gun pointing at him like it was, he couldn't really do anything about it.

Be honest, he told himself. There was nothing he could do anyway, even if he wasn't covered.

The bank president's normally beefy face was pale with fear now. He said hurriedly, "All right, all right. Don't shoot. I'll open the vault."

"Figured you would," the boss outlaw said. His voice was full of contempt.

The bank president shuffled toward an open door between the desks and the tellers' cages. Beyond it, the vault door was visible. While that was going on, two of the outlaws carrying canvas bags moved behind the cages to empty the money from the tellers' drawers. Logan couldn't help but wince a little as he saw one of the men reach for the pouch of coins he had laid on the counter a few minutes earlier. All the money he had saved was about to disappear into one of those bags of loot.

That was when the bank's front door opened again. The man who walked inside was young, with an open, friendly, unsuspecting face. He wore a badge pinned to the lapel of his coat. He stopped short a couple of steps inside the lobby, looked around at the outlaws regarding him with shocked, frozen stares, and then fumbled at the butt of the pistol holstered on his hip.

Another duster-clad outlaw, but this one without a mask over his face, rushed into the bank behind the lawman and shouted, "Look out, boys! A deputy!"

Logan knew instantly what had happened. The gang had left one man outside to hold their horses and keep a lookout for anybody or anything that might interrupt the robbery. But the sixth man had fallen down on the job, probably gotten overconfident, and somehow had let a deputy walk right past him into the bank.

The young lawman cleared leather, but before he could bring his gun to bear on any of the bank robbers, the lookout shoved the muzzle of a long-barreled Remington against his back and pulled the trigger. The .44 caliber ball ripped through the deputy's body and exploded out the front of his chest in a spray of blood and torn flesh. The shot's impact pitched the young man forward on his face, more than likely dead by the time he hit the floor.

That lethal commotion distracted the rest of the robbers, and the bank president found some gumption again. He lunged at the boss outlaw, grabbed his gun hand, and tried to wrestle the revolver away from him. The gun boomed and the bank president staggered back as he clutched at his midsection.

"Those shots'll bring the law down on us!" one of the men who'd been emptying the tellers' cages cried. "Let's get the hell out of here!"

They started to rush past the customers, but then one of the duster-clad desperadoes paused and reached out with his left arm to grab Logan.

"They won't shoot at us if we got a cripple for a shield!" the man shouted to his companions.

Logan wasn't so sure about that. He didn't want to catch a stray bullet. But even if the outlaw was right, Logan's instincts reacted instantly to being grabbed like that. As the robber wrapped his arm around his neck, Logan thrust his cane backward between the man's legs and twisted.

That threw the robber off-balance and made him fall forward against Logan's back. Still clutching the cane, Logan drove the elbow of his good arm into the man's stomach. That broke the outlaw's grip. Logan stumbled forward a step and turned around.

Gasping for breath from the blow to his belly, the man tried to bring his gun up for a shot at Logan. As the barrel came level with him, Logan didn't stop to think about what he was doing. He flung out his left arm. His wrist hit the inside of the outlaw's wrist and knocked the gun aside just as the man pulled the trigger. The revolver roared and spouted flame, but the bullet smacked harmlessly into the counter at the tellers' cages.

Logan swung the cane with his other hand and cracked the hardwood shaft against the side of the outlaw's head. The blow made the man's eyes roll up in their sockets. The gun slipped from his fingers and thudded to the floor. His knees folded up and dropped him. He was out cold.

"Look out, mister!" one of the other customers yelled.

Logan jerked his head around and saw that the rest of the gang had paused in their headlong flight toward the door. Their guns came up, and Logan found himself staring down the weapons' barrels at sudden, smashing death.

10.

The only thing Logan could do was drop to the floor as the outlaws opened fire on him. Gun-thunder filled the bank's lobby and echoed back deafeningly from the walls.

The first volley passed several feet over Logan's recumbent form and smashed into the wall. The customers and the tellers who had been prodded into the corner had already started to scatter and dive for cover. Logan hoped no one was hit, but he didn't have time to worry much about it.

He reached out with his right hand and scooped up the gun that the unconscious outlaw had dropped.

Although Logan had always been left-handed – his folks hadn't tried to force him out of it, as many parents did with their left-handed youngsters – he had fired a gun with his right hand plenty of times before. He wasn't a two-gun man like some pistoleers, but he had practiced the border shift. Cocking the hammer and squeezing the trigger didn't seem too unnatural as he angled the barrel up from the floor.

His first shot hit one of the outlaws in the hip and knocked him into the man beside him. Logan fired another round that left a bloody line on the cheek of another man.

Another gun started to bark. One of the customers had pulled a pocket pistol from under his coat and now joined the fray. He sprayed several slugs around the outlaws.

Facing that much opposition, and with time running out on them, the robbers' nerve broke. They turned and bolted out the door, even the man Logan had wounded, although he was staggering as his leg tried to fold up under him. The five men disappeared.

But a heartbeat later more shots roared right outside the bank. The building's front windows shattered. A shotgun boomed.

"Everybody get down and stay down!" Logan shouted at the men in the bank. The ones who weren't already on the floor hit it in a hurry.

A few more bullets whistled through the lobby and struck the walls as the gun battle continued outside. Then an abrupt silence fell. It was broken after a few seconds by an agonized moan, then some raspy, bitter cursing that faded away to nothing.

With a heavy step, a burly man appeared in the doorway and swung a double-barreled Greener from right to left so that he covered the whole lobby.

"Any more of 'em in here?" he called.

Logan placed the revolver he had used on the floor and slid it away from him. Then he held up his empty hand and said, "There's one over here, Sheriff, but he's unconscious."

He had spotted a badge on the newcomer's coat.

The lawman hurried over and pointed the scattergun at the unconscious outlaw. "What happened to him?"

The customer who had taken out a pistol and started shooting pointed a finger at Logan and said, "That fella there walloped him with a cane."

Logan struggled to get up. One of the tellers came over to help him, taking his good arm to support him.

The sheriff or marshal or whatever he was looked around and asked, "Anybody else hurt in here?"

"Mr. Skelling," another teller said as he knelt beside the fallen bank president. "He was shot."

"And poor Randy's dead, from the looks of it," the lawman said as he frowned down at the deputy who'd been shot in the back. He sighed. "I reckon those idiots in the dusters tried to hold up the bank?"

"They would have, if not for Deputy Porter and this gentleman," said the teller who was bracing Logan up. "He's a real hero, Marshal Radcliffe."

Logan didn't want anybody calling him a hero. Anyone who knew some of the things he had done in the past would never think that of him.

Right now, though, he didn't really care. He was shaky and wanted to sit down.

"If somebody could . . . get me a chair," he said.

One of the men did that, bringing a desk chair from behind the railing, and Logan sank gratefully into it.

A couple more deputies came into the bank. One of them shook his head at the sight of his murdered comrade and asked, "What do we do about all those bodies out on the street, Marshal?"

Radcliffe, a red-faced man with a goatee, snapped, "Send for the damn undertaker, blast it! And fetch a doctor for Mr. Skelling, too, while you're at it." He turned back to the men who had been in the bank when the would-be robbers burst in and went on, "Now somebody tell me what the devil happened in here."

Several of them tried to tell it at once. Radcliffe shouted them down and started asking questions. Logan didn't pay much attention to any of the conversation. He sat with his hands clasped between his knees and his head down as he tried to catch his breath.

Finally the marshal asked him, "What's your name, mister?"

Logan had been dreading that question. He wished he could have gotten out of there before Radcliffe asked it. If anyone in Hot Springs was likely to recognize his name, it would be a lawman. But he didn't see how he could refuse to answer or even lie. He had given his name to too many people in town for that.

"It's Logan Handley," he said quietly.

"Handley . . ." Radcliffe repeated. "Seems I've heard that name before. Lemme have a look at you, Mr. Handley."

Logan lifted his head. Radcliffe stared down at him for a long moment. The lawman frowned.

"Yeah, I've seen you before, I know it. Can't recollect where, but it'll come to me – " Radcliffe stopped short, then exclaimed, "Santa Fe! About four years ago, it was. I was a deputy there when you had that run-in with Dave Bardwell and his bunch! Logan Handley! Sure!"

Logan didn't see any point in denying it. He remembered very well how Bardwell and three other gunnies working for a rival of the cattleman who had hired him had cornered him in a dance hall. That had been quite a stampede as the dancers tried to clear the floor before the bullets started to fly. When the smoke cleared, Bardwell and his three companions had been on the floor, bleeding their lives out, while Logan was still on his feet, albeit with a couple of nicks. He had never shot faster or straighter than that night. If Marshal Radcliffe had been packing a badge in Santa Fe at the time, Logan could see how he would remember the incident.

"You were one hell of a pistol *ar-teest*, amigo," Radcliffe continued. "Some folks said you were as fast with a gun as Hickock. What happened to you?"

"Life," Logan said. That just brought a puzzled stare to Radcliffe's face, but Logan ignored it. With a gesture, he asked one of the men to hand him his cane. When he had hold of it, he said, "Can I go now?"

"Why, sure, I reckon I've got the story, or enough of it, anyway," the marshal said. "You may have to testify at the inquest, though. That be all right with you?"

Logan pushed himself to his feet and leaned on the cane.

"As long as I can get time off at the barber shop," he said.

That made Radcliffe and the other men in the bank stare at him even more. They didn't know whether to be afraid of him, since they now knew that he was a famous gunman, or to feel sorry for him since those days obviously were behind him. Neither of those things made Logan feel any better.

He started to limp out of the bank, then stopped and turned back. His pouch of coins still lay on the counter. All the bullets that had flown around the tellers' cages, and none of them had struck the pouch.

"Would someone hand me that?" he asked.

One of the tellers fetched it, the one who had started to wait on Logan, in fact. The man said, "You don't want to deposit it anymore?"

Logan took the pouch, stuck it in his pocket, and said, "I'm not sure this bank is safe."

He felt all their eyes on him as he stumped out.

* * *

Despite the gray clouds scudding through the sky and the chill in the air, Logan was sweating by the time he got back to the boarding house. Doc would be expecting him at the barber shop and he hated to disappoint a man he had come to consider a friend, but he had to think things through and figure out his next move.

A ball of sick fear rolled around in his stomach. The bloody sensationalism of the botched bank robbery insured that news of it would be all over town in no time. More than half a dozen men had heard Marshal Radcliffe announce that the cripple who worked in the barber shop was really Logan Handley, the famous gunfighter. They would talk about it, too, to anyone who would listen. Logan was sure of that.

How long would it be before someone who wanted him dead heard about it?

Vengeful gunmen were going to start gathering around Hot Springs like vultures . . .

"Mr. Handley, what are you doing here in the middle of the day?" Vickie Eastland asked from the parlor as Logan limped into the foyer.

He didn't particularly want to explain, but when she saw how pale and shaken he was, she hurried out of the parlor and took hold of his arm.

"Here, you should sit down and rest," she told him. "Don't try to climb the stairs to your room yet."

He couldn't deny that he wasn't in very good shape at that moment, mentally or physically. He allowed Vickie to steer him into the parlor, and they sat down on the divan. She kept plenty of distance between them, but still, this was the most intimate they had been with each other since the night she had rubbed his neck and shoulder.

And Logan remembered how that had ended.

"What's wrong? Why aren't you at the barber shop?"

He knew she would find out the truth anyway. Some of the other boarders would carry the news when they came back to the house, and even if they didn't, Vickie was bound to hear about it the next time she went to the market. He swallowed and said, "There was a bank robbery . . . an attempted bank robbery . . . and I got caught in the middle of it."

She put a hand to her mouth and said, "Good Lord! Were you hurt?"

"Not really. I – "

Before Logan could go on, the front door burst open and Rusty Turner rushed into the foyer. He spotted Logan and Vickie in the parlor and swung toward them.

"There you are!" he said. "When I heard about it, I went to the barber shop, but Doc told me you never came back from lunch. Dadgum it, Logan, I never knowed you was a gunfighter! Never even suspected it!"

"A gunfighter?" Vickie echoed as her eyebrows rose.

"You bet," Rusty continued, practically bubbling over with enthusiasm. "People are talkin' about it all over downtown. I heard all about how Logan shot it out with those owlhoots and ran 'em out of the bank – right into the gunsights of Marshal Radcliffe and his deputies! Blood was ever'where, folks are sayin'. Runnin' in the streets like rain. Never figured one of your boarders would turn out to be a famous shootist, did you, Miz Eastland?"

Vickie looked both horrified and angry, Logan thought, but her voice was cool and steady as she replied, "No, Mr. Turner, I didn't. And I certainly wouldn't have expected it of Mr. Handley here."

Logan could only sit there, numb and silent, as Rusty went on, "I should'a recognized the name. He's been in gunfights all over the West. Faced down some of the most dangerous men there was. Logan, how many have you killed?"

As much as he liked Rusty, right now Logan wanted to clench his good hand into a fist and pound it into the garrulous veteran's face. Anything to shut him up.

Instead Logan said, "To tell you the truth, I don't know. I don't dwell on it."

"But Rusty is telling the truth?" Vickie said. "You shot it out with those bank robbers, and in the past you . . ."

"I hired out my gun, yes. And those outlaws were going to shoot me. I just defended myself."

"But how – " She stopped herself short.

"How did a cripple fight a bunch of bank robbers? Instinct. Habit." His voice hardened. "When you know you're going to die, you do what you have to to stop it."

She didn't say anything in response to that, but he noticed that she had drawn even farther way on the divan.

There was nothing unusual about that reaction. He had seen it plenty of times in the past.

After a moment, he said, "If you're worried about the reputation of your place, I can move out. I can understand why you'd feel that way."

For a moment she seemed to consider the offer, but then she shook her head.

"I can't ask you to do that," she said. "You've been a good boarder, always paid on time, followed my rules, never caused any trouble. It wouldn't be right for me to ask you to leave."

Rusty said, "Shoot, havin' the famous Logan Handley livin' here will just draw more folks."

That was exactly the problem, thought Logan. Infamous or notorious would be better words to describe him, and the attention he would draw to the boarding house would be the wrong sort. Some of the folks looking for him would want to kill him, and if he stayed here, there was a good chance someone would get hurt.

Someone innocent.

Someone like Vickie Eastland.

He couldn't allow that to happen.

But in order to move out of the boarding house and into a hotel, he would have to have more money. And that wouldn't be a long-term solution, either, since he would just be trading one set of potential innocent victims for another. He needed to find a place of his own, or else he had to leave Hot Springs.

He couldn't do that without finding out whether or not Dr. August Strittmatter actually could help him. That wouldn't come cheap, either.

But he still had something to sell, he realized. He had a reputation. And he wasn't totally without gun-handling skill, even right-handed. He realized now that he had been going about this all the wrong way. He had been drifting and feeling sorry for himself, when what he should have been doing was taking what he still had and using it.

He leaned his weight on the cane and levered himself to his feet.

"Where are you going?" Vickie asked.

"Upstairs."

She stood up as well and said, "You're not going to pack or anything foolish like that, are you?"

She didn't want him to leave, he realized. He wasn't sure why she felt that way, but evidently she did. He smiled and said, "Not just yet. I have to do some thinking."

"Are you going back to the barber shop?" Rusty asked.

"Not today. Tell Doc that I'm sorry, would you?"

"Sure. I know he'd hate to lose you, Logan. He told me he's enjoyed havin' you around." Rusty paused. "And I reckon it'd be good for his business if you kept on workin' there, too."

Of course it would. What fat, middle-aged storekeeper wouldn't want to have his hair clippings swept up by a famous gunfighter?

"We'll see," Logan said. He limped out of the parlor and turned toward the stairs.

As he did, he felt the hard lump of the money pouch in his pocket. Just as well that he hadn't deposited those coins after all, he told himself.

First thing tomorrow morning, he needed to go out and see about buying a gun.

11.

Logan slept late the next morning. No dead men had danced through his dreams, but he seemed to see large, crimson pools of blood in the street outside the bank. When he woke and sat up to scrub his good hand over his face, he knew that blood came from the robbers who had been cut down by Marshal Radcliffe and the other deputies. Those deaths weren't on his conscience, Logan told himself. He hadn't killed any of those men.

But they had died only a few steps away from him, after he had traded shots with them. Just being in the same vicinity with him seemed to bring death along with it.

One more good reason to find another place to live.

"Breakfast is already over," Vickie told him when he went downstairs, "but there's still coffee on the stove and I put aside a couple of biscuits for you."

Her expression and voice were neutral, as if she would have done the same for any boarder, even one who had just moved in. Which she probably would have, Logan thought. He knew better than to read anything into the gesture.

"Thank you," he said, just as coolly polite as she was. "I'll help myself."

"You'll have to. I have laundry to take care of."

He went into the kitchen, poured the coffee, and sat down at the small table in there to eat the biscuits.

Vickie had done more than just set them aside for him, though. She'd left a jar of peach preserves beside the plate. Logan had to smile a little at that.

He had just finished eating when Rusty came into the kitchen, seemingly in a hurry as usual.

"Miz Eastland told me she thought you were in here," Rusty said. "My boss wants to see you, Logan."

That announcement put a puzzled frown on Logan's face.

"You work for Marcus Baldwin, the timber baron. I've heard a lot about him."

It would have been impossible to be around Hot Springs for very long without hearing about Marcus Baldwin, even if he hadn't been friends with Rusty. The man owned vast stretches of timberland where a veritable army of loggers worked, harvesting the natural wealth, and if that wasn't enough, he also operated the freight company for which Rusty labored as a driver. Rumor had it that he was involved in other businesses as well. He had a reputation as a ruthless, but not necessarily dishonest, man.

But most people wouldn't have been too surprised, either, to discover that some of his dealings were on the shady side.

Logan looked up at Rusty and went on, "What in the world does he want with me?"

"Now, that I couldn't tell you," Rusty said. "Mr. Baldwin had his private secretary find me and ask me to bring you to the office, though, as soon as I could. I went by the barber shop, since I didn't know whether or not I'd find you there, but Doc told me you hadn't been in. That's when I figured you were probably here."

He wouldn't have been in just a little while, Logan thought. He still intended to see about buying a gun today. But he supposed he could go see Marcus Baldwin first. Chances were that he wouldn't need to be armed for that.

He smiled a little to himself and hoped that he hadn't jinxed the meeting by thinking that.

He drank the rest of the coffee in his cup, set it on the table, and got to his feet with the help of his cane.

"All right," he told Rusty. "Let's go."

The offices of the Baldwin Timber Company and the Baldwin Freight Line occupied a one-story building of brown sandstone a couple of blocks from the bank where the shootout had occurred the previous day. Next to the building was a large wooden barn with a spacious corral on the other side of it that served as the freight line's wagon yard.

Rusty took Logan into the building, where a clerk led them along a corridor to the door to Marcus Baldwin's private office. The man told Rusty, "All right, Turner, you can go now."

"Don't I need to stay with Logan?" Rusty asked. "I was sent to fetch him, after all."

"And so you have," the clerk said coldly. "I assure you, we can take care of Mr. Handley from this point."

"Well, all right," Rusty said with obvious reluctance. To Logan, he added, "I don't have to leave on a run today, so I'll be next door at the barn if you need me."

Logan nodded and said, "All right. Thanks, Rusty."

Rusty left grudgingly. Logan knew he wanted to find out what was going on so he could spread the word. As fond as he was of Rusty, Logan thought that maybe a little discretion would be better, so he was glad he would be meeting with Baldwin alone.

He was still extremely curious what the businessman wanted with him, though. But he would be finding out soon, he thought as the clerk opened the door.

An outer office lay beyond it, with another door leading to Marcus Baldwin's private sanctum. A thin man who looked like he was made out of steel and whalebone stood up from behind the desk in the outer office and said, "Mr. Handley? I'm Charles Stroud, Mr. Baldwin's private secretary. Please come in."

Stroud didn't offer to shake hands. Instead he turned to the other door, rapped bony knuckles on it, and opened it to say, "Mr. Handley is here as you requested, sir."

Logan heard a powerful, resonant voice say, "Bring him on in, Stroud."

The private secretary stood aside from the door and gestured for Logan to precede him.

Logan stepped into an opulent office paneled in dark wood. A large desk dominated the room. A table with a map spread out on it stood to one side. More maps were mounted on the walls in gilt frames. Logan wondered if they represented Baldwin's timber holdings.

Marcus Baldwin himself was impressive as well as he stood up and extended a hand across the desk. Dressed in an expensive gray tweed suit, he was medium height, broad-shouldered, and looked like he might have swung a double-bitted ax himself in his younger days. A mane of gray and silver hair framed a face that wouldn't have been out of place on a Roman coin.

"Mr. Handley," he said as Logan shook with him. "A pleasure to meet you. I'm Marcus Baldwin."

"Logan Handley," Logan introduced himself, even though Baldwin obviously knew his name already.

Baldwin waved him into a chair plushly upholstered in brown leather that stood in front of the desk and said,

"Please, have a seat." As the two men settled down in their chairs, Baldwin went on, "I should say that it's an honor to meet you, sir, as well as a pleasure, after what you did yesterday. I have a considerable amount of money on deposit in that bank, and I hate to think of it being cleaned out by those would-be thieves. I understand you deserve most of the credit for stopping them."

Logan folded his hands on the head of his cane and said, "I'm not sure how much truth there is to that, Mr. Baldwin. I was more concerned with keeping them from dragging me out into the street as a hostage. I had a hunch that a lot of bullets might start flying around . . . and I was right."

"Yes, from what I hear Marshal Radcliffe and his deputies were quite prompt once the shooting started. None of the bandits escaped except the one you rendered unconscious."

"No, sir, they didn't."

"Well, on behalf of myself and everyone else who has money in the bank, thank you for what you did."

"I appreciate that, but I was more worried about saving my own skin."

Baldwin waved that off with a well-manicured hand and said, "I've heard about your medical problems, Mr. Handley. You have my sympathy."

Logan managed not to bristle at that comment. He hadn't asked for sympathy from anyone since the disease had struck him down that night in Aspen Creek. He didn't want it. But he nodded, appearing to acknowledge Baldwin's words politely without actually saying anything.

"I'm sure it must be difficult for a man like you to have to face such things," Baldwin went on.

"What do you mean by that?" Logan asked.

"A man accustomed to being active, to *doing* things."

"I have a job," Logan said. "Two of them, in fact."

He didn't know if he would be going back to the barber shop or to Dumont's, but he still considered himself employed at both places for the time being.

Baldwin chuckled and shook his head. "I hope you won't be offended by this, Mr. Handley, but when I heard about what happened at the bank I did a little looking into your background. You don't strike me as the sort of man who would be happy working in a barber shop or tending bar. That seems like a waste of your particular skills. I was wondering if you might be willing to take on a little job for me."

Logan had had conversations similar to this with rich men in the past, but that had been when he was hale and fit. He said, "I don't see what I could do for you, Mr. Baldwin. I'm sure you've noticed that I'm . . . not the man I once was."

"On the contrary, your actions in the bank yesterday prove that you're still the same man inside, despite the physical problems you've had to go through," Baldwin said. "And with the money I'm prepared to pay you, you'd be better able to afford treatment for your condition. Again, no offense, but you can't be making much at Dumont's and Doc Reese's."

In Logan's experience, a man who made a habit of prefacing his statements with *No offense* didn't really give a damn if he offended anyone or not. That was doubly true when a man was wealthy like Marcus Baldwin.

But despite that, Baldwin was right about one thing: even working two jobs, it was going to take Logan a long time to save up enough money for the treatments he wanted. That was time he didn't have. So he was curious enough – and desperate enough – to ask, "What sort of job are you talking about?"

"I'm sending a shipment of money on the train to Little Rock. It's the payroll for one of my mills up there. To be honest with you, I'm worried about the safety of that money. You may not be aware of it, but there have been a number of train robberies in this area in recent months." Baldwin made a face and shook his head. "That blasted Jesse James and his brother and cousins. The whole family is just a bunch of criminals! And yet people tend to glorify them. Common criminals, and otherwise law-abiding people help them hide from the authorities."

Logan didn't mention that he had had his own encounter with Jesse James on his way to Hot Springs, and he didn't want to argue about what had led Jesse and his relations to start riding the owlhoot trail in the first place.

Instead he said, "That's the sort of job I used to take from time to time. I've ridden herd on more than one payroll. But that was a different time."

He looked meaningfully at his withered left arm, and then at his cane and right leg.

Baldwin leaned forward in his chair, clasped his hands together on the desk, and said, "On the contrary, I believe that your actions in the bank yesterday prove that you're still capable of doing what needs to be done, regardless of your physical limitations. You possess qualities that are equally important: experience, instinct, and nerves that are cool under fire."

Maybe Baldwin was right, Logan thought. He had told himself that he needed to start making better use of his skills again. That was one reason he had planned to buy a gun today. And yet at the first opportunity, he had let self-doubt crop up again. He had insisted that failure was inevitable, when as a matter of fact he didn't know if that was true.

Those thoughts were going through his mind and he was leaning toward accepting, but Baldwin didn't know that. The timber magnate must have thought Logan needed some more convincing, because he said, "There's another reason I want to hire you, Mr. Handley. Something more precious to me than any amount of money will be on that train tomorrow. My daughter Gillian is going to Little Rock, too."

"Are you talking about me again, Father?" a female voice asked from behind Logan. He turned slightly in the chair to look back over his shoulder and saw a young woman coming into the room. He hadn't even heard her open the door. That was how graceful she was.

Not to mention beautiful. Her skin was creamy, and her features were as perfect as any to be found in a cameo. Waves of pale blond hair framed her face. She was even more lovely when she smiled, like she did when she held out her hand and said, "You must be Mr. Handley. I'm Gillian Baldwin, and my father tells me that you're going to be accompanying me on my trip to Little Rock."

12.

Sounding somewhat embarrassed, Baldwin said, "Mr. Handley hasn't actually agreed to take the job yet, my dear."

"Do you think spending time with me would be a *job*, Mr. Handley?" Gillian asked. Logan heard the faint tone of mockery in her voice but didn't know if it was directed at him or her father . . . or at both of them. He had encountered many young, extremely beautiful women in his life – none more beautiful than Gillian Baldwin, though, he thought – and most of them seemed to consider the world to be their own personal playground. And men, for the most part, were nothing but their toys.

However, he didn't know Gillian Baldwin nearly well enough to say whether she shared those attitudes, and it probably wasn't fair of him to assume that she did. He said, "I think that accompanying you just about anywhere would be a pleasure, Miss Baldwin. A distinct pleasure."

"Well, then, why hesitate? Say yes and take Father's money. That's what everyone else does."

"Really, Gillian – " Baldwin began.

"Besides," she went on, ignoring him, "Father refuses to let me go to Little Rock unless I have a suitable traveling companion, and I really need to do some shopping. Little Rock isn't exactly Paris or Boston, but the shopping there *is* better than here in Hot Springs. Please say you'll come with me, Mr. Handley."

"How can I refuse?" Logan heard himself saying.

He wasn't sure where the words came from; he hadn't made a conscious decision to accept the job. But that's what he had done, and now he was bound by it.

"We haven't discussed compensation yet," Baldwin said.

"Whatever you were going to offer him, double it," Gillian said. "I think that's fair, don't you, Mr. Handley?"

"Wages aren't the sort of thing proper young women discuss," Baldwin said. The words came out a little tightly because his jaw was clenched with annoyance.

Gillian smiled at Logan again, cocked one carefully plucked and arched eyebrow, and said, "My father is the one who claims I'm proper, Mr. Handley, not me." As Baldwin opened his mouth to say something else, she forestalled him with a raised hand and went on, "That's all right, I'm going. One more thing, though . . . There's going to be a party at my father's house this evening, and I think you should attend, Mr. Handley. That will give us a chance to get to know each other better before we leave for Little Rock."

Baldwin nodded and said, "That's actually a good idea. There are a few other minor matters I'd like to discuss with you, Logan. You don't mind if I call you Logan, do you?"

Actually, the assumption of familiarity did rub Logan the wrong way, but he wasn't going to say that. Instead he said, "That's fine. I don't see any reason why I can't be there." He would have to get out some of his better clothes and hope they hadn't gotten too wrinkled from being packed away. Maybe Vickie wouldn't mind ironing them. He could pay her extra for the job . . .

"I'll see you tonight, Logan," Gillian said. She hadn't asked for his permission to call him by his given name.

Logan doubted if she asked permission for most of the things she did.

When she was gone, Baldwin said, "I'll pay you three hundred dollars for the trip."

Logan didn't know if that would be enough to get him started with treatments from Dr. Strittmatter, but it seemed entirely possible that it would be. Besides, he had never liked haggling. He nodded and said, "All right."

Baldwin stood up, and so did Logan, although not so easily. They shook hands again, and Baldwin said, "Of course, that fee is contingent on my daughter's safe return to Hot Springs. No offense . . ."

There was that phrase again.

Baldwin smiled, but his eyes were hard as flint as he went on, "If you don't bring her back safely to me, Mr. Handley, it would be smarter for you if you just kept going."

* * *

Logan found Rusty in the big barn next to the office building, where the teamster had said he would be.

"What was it the boss wanted with you?" Rusty asked bluntly.

"He offered me a job."

Rusty looked confused. "What sort of job?"

"Guarding a payroll shipment on the train to Little Rock . . . and guarding his daughter as well."

A low whistle came from Rusty's pursed lips. He said, "Miss Gillian is the best-lookin' gal in all of Hot Springs. Maybe in all of Arkansas!"

Logan laughed. "I couldn't say one way or the other about that. I haven't seen all the women in Arkansas, or even in Hot Springs, for that matter. I can't deny that she's pretty easy on the eyes, though."

"Easy on the eyes," Rusty repeated. He snorted. "That's like sayin' it's hot in the desert or cold at the North Pole!" Rusty paused, then frowned. "You said he offered you the job. Did you take it?"

"I did," Logan said. "I'll have to tell Doc and Dewey that I won't be coming in anymore."

"They'll be disappointed, I reckon, but shoot . . . gettin' paid to spend time with Gillian Baldwin! No man could turn that down. No man in his right mind, anyway."

"Of course, I also have to protect that payroll from Jesse James or any other bandit who takes it into his head to rob the train we'll be on."

"Yeah." Rusty scratched his jaw. "How do you plan on goin' about that?"

"I was hoping you could point me in the direction of a good gunsmith," Logan said.

As it turned out, Rusty was able to do more than that. Not surprisingly, since he seemed to know just about everyone in Hot Springs, he had a friend who sold and worked on guns.

Buck Finnerty was a wiry man with dark hair and a mustache. He had a canvas apron dotted with gun oil stains over his butternut shirt. After Rusty introduced them, Finnerty said, "I heard about that bank robbery yesterday, Mr. Handley. I reckon just about the whole town did. Might even be in the papers in Little Rock and St. Louis by next week."

Logan made an effort not to wince at that comment. Having his name in the newspapers was just about the last thing he wanted, but he didn't see any way he could stop it from happening. Journalistic efforts took on a life of their own and spread far and wide sometimes.

"What can I do for you?" Finnerty went on.

"I need to buy a gun," Logan said. "I'm left-handed, and I don't know if you've noticed – " He smiled to take any sting out of the words. "I'm not exactly as nimble with that hand as I used to be."

"But you can shoot just fine with your right, from what I heard about that dust-up with those robbers," Finnerty said.

"I can shoot with my right. I wouldn't say I'm that good with it. But I don't have much choice in the matter, so I was thinking maybe a Colt Single Action Army with the shorter barrel. It's fairly easy to handle."

Finnerty nodded. "I can fix you up with one of those, all right. Probably be a good belt gun for you." He frowned in thought for a moment. "But I've got somethin' else you might want to take a look at."

He rummaged around under the long counter in his shop for a moment and came up with a wooden case about two feet long and a foot wide. He set it on the counter, snapped the latches, and swung the lid up to reveal a sawed-off shotgun. The twin, blued steel barrels were a foot long, extending out from a polished, gleaming stock that had been fashioned into a pistol grip. The weapon was only about eighteen inches from one end to the other.

"I made this special for a fella, and he up and died before he could pay me for it," Finnerty explained. "He was a bounty hunter, and he didn't care much whether he brought in the men he was after dead or alive. Not to speak ill of the dead, but he had a habit of sneakin' up behind somebody and puttin' a bullet in 'em. He figured this'd do an even better job of it. Never got to try it out, though. Somebody snuck up on *him* instead."

Logan couldn't help but chuckle despite the grim nature of what Finnerty had just said. He had known several bounty hunters in his time and knew that some of them weren't much better than the men they pursued. Of course, neither was he.

"How heavy is it?" he asked.

Finnerty pushed the case across the counter and invited, "See for yourself."

Using his right hand, Logan picked up the shotgun. It was a hefty weapon, but his right arm was plenty strong. It just wasn't quite as deft as his left arm had been before he had fallen ill.

"Try the action," Finnerty suggested.

Logan pulled back the hammers, pointed the shotgun at the wall, and squeezed each trigger in turn. He could tell that the action was smooth.

Rusty said, "That'd blow the hell outta somebody as long as they weren't more'n ten or twenty feet away."

"Yep, it sure would," Finnerty said. "You won't find anything better for close work, Mr. Handley."

"I think you're right," Logan said.

"I could rig you a holster for it, too. Carry it on your right leg, and pack the Colt cross-draw."

Logan nodded. Finnerty's suggestions were good ones. With that much firepower, he would stand a better chance in any fight.

"I'm not sure I can afford such a fine weapon as this."

Finnerty grinned and said, "Shoot, I'll make you a good price on it, Mr. Handley. Havin' a man like you usin' one of my guns . . . it'd be an honor."

Logan made a decision. He said, "Can you have everything ready for me tomorrow morning?" The train for Little Rock pulled out at ten o'clock, Marcus Baldwin had told him.

"Sure."

"I'll pick it up around nine. I want the case for the

shotgun, as well as the holster." There would be times when he didn't want to carry the sawed-off openly, thought Logan. "I'll need ammunition for both guns, too."

"You bet." Finnerty added up the total for everything.

"I'll pay you in the morning," Logan said. He could get the money from Baldwin at the party that night. Under the circumstances, Baldwin probably wouldn't object to letting him have an advance on his wages.

"Sounds mighty fine. It's a pleasure doin' business with you, Mr. Handley."

"Same here," Logan said.

He found that he was looking forward to having the weight of a gun on his hip again. And the smooth wooden stock of the sawed-off against his palm had been very satisfying. For a man who had made his living with a gun for so long to be unarmed . . . well, it just wasn't natural.

"Thanks for your help with this, Rusty," Logan said as they left Buck Finnerty's shop.

"I was mighty glad to do it," Rusty said. "That shotgun's really somethin', ain't it? When you get on that train tomorrow, you're gonna be armed for bear!"

Logan thought about Jesse James and said, "It's not bears I'm worried about."

13.

Back in his room at the boarding house, Logan set his valise on the bed, opened it, and took out his best shirt and his vest. His suit was already hanging up in the wardrobe, and as he studied his shirt he decided it would be all right to wear to the party at the Baldwin house. Marcus Baldwin had promised to send a carriage for him at seven o'clock.

Logan got his suit from the wardrobe and laid it out on the bed, just to be sure it was still clean and pressed enough to wear, and while he was doing that he heard footsteps in the hall. They paused just outside his open door.

"Do you need some laundry done, Mr. Handley?" Vickie asked. "I can have it picked up with the rest."

Vickie washed the bedding for the house herself and hung it to dry in the back yard. Her clothing and that of the boarders was picked up once a week by a Chinese man whose family operated a laundry several blocks away.

"No, that's all right," Logan told her. "I just wanted to make sure my good clothes were all right for tonight, and I think they are."

"Tonight?" Vickie repeated. "What's tonight?"

For a second Logan wished he hadn't said anything, but he supposed it didn't really matter. Vickie would know something was going on when the carriage arrived that evening, plus there was the fact that he would be leaving for Little Rock in the morning.

"I've been invited to a party," he said.

"Oh?" She smiled. "At the barber shop?"

"At Marcus Baldwin's house."

That put a definite look of surprise on her face. She said, "Marcus Baldwin? The man Rusty works for?"

"That's right. And I work for him, too, now."

"Driving a freight wagon?"

Logan shook his head. "Guarding the payroll for his lumber mill. And his daughter."

Vickie drew in a breath and said, "Gillian."

"You know her?"

"Everyone in Little Rock knows Gillian Baldwin. Just like they know her father. It's impossible not to know those timber barons."

Baldwin was the only timber baron Logan was aware of, but he supposed there were other men in the same business. He said, "Miss Baldwin is going to Little Rock on the train tomorrow, so I guess this gathering tonight is something of a going-away party for her. Although I don't think she intends to be gone for very long. She mentioned she wanted to do some shopping down there, but that's all."

"And you'll be traveling on the train with her."

"Her father is worried about holdups," Logan said with a shrug. "He doesn't want anything happening to her, or to his money."

"Yes, I imagine he'd have a hard time choosing between them if he had to."

Vickie's tone of voice and the look on her face made Logan say, "I take it you don't care for the Baldwins."

"As a rule I'm not fond of rich people who think

they're better than everyone else. People who think they can get whatever they want just by demanding it." It was Vickie's turn to shrug as she went on, "But I suppose I don't have anything *personally* against Marcus Baldwin and his daughter. I just don't like their . . . their circle of society."

"All right," Logan said.

"But if you want to be part of it, that's fine."

"I'm not part of it," he said. "I've worked for plenty of rich people, but that's it. I'm not one of them. I'm just a hired hand."

"A hired gun-hand."

"I'm not denying it," he said in a flat voice. Vickie's disapproval of him was starting to wear thin. He didn't know what had happened between her and her former husband to make her so bitter, and he didn't care. He hadn't been part of it.

She turned toward the door but paused to ask, "Will you be here for supper?"

"Mr. Baldwin didn't say anything about me joining them for dinner, so I suppose so. He's sending a carriage for me at seven."

"I'll be sure we're finished eating in plenty of time, then. We wouldn't want you to be late. Miss Baldwin might be disappointed if you were."

"Maybe so," Logan said.

But he doubted it. Gillian had seemed to enjoy flirting with him, but he figured that she didn't really give him a second thought.

* * *

The Baldwin mansion was located atop one of the hills that surrounded Little Rock. The carriage followed a road that twisted back and forth as it climbed the wooded slopes. From the window Logan saw the lights of the town spread out along the valley below him.

Supper at the boarding house had been a rather strained affair. Some of the boarders picked up on the tension and were quieter than usual.

Not Rusty, of course. He was as full of talk as ever, this time about Logan going to work for Marcus Baldwin. Logan was grateful that Rusty didn't say much about Gillian. He suspected that would have just irritated Vickie even more.

Vickie was acting like she was jealous, which made no sense. Other than that one moment she had never shown any signs of being interested in Logan. He was certain that Gillian wasn't, either.

It would be foolish for either of them to set her sights on him. He wasn't exactly what any woman would regard as a catch. A crippled gunman with enemies who were bound to show up looking for him sooner or later . . . No woman in her right mind would want that much to do with him.

The carriage was fancy, which came as no surprise. Lots of gleaming black wood and brasswork, pulled by a team of fine black horses with silver-decorated harness and feathered plumes attached to their heads. Plumes! Logan thought it was all a little ridiculous, but he knew rich people liked such extravagances. If he'd ever been rich, maybe he would have, too.

The hilltop where the mansion sat had been leveled off, but many of the trees remained. The big house was ablaze with lights as it sat at the end of a short lane paved with crushed stone. It had three stories, Logan saw as the carriage approached and then turned into an area where a number of other carriages were parked. Tall white columns flanked the entrance. The place wasn't built exactly like a plantation house, he thought, but it came closer to that than anything else.

The driver, who hadn't said a word to Logan so far, climbed down from the high seat and opened the door for him. Logan climbed out, which was something of an awkward process with his bad leg. Getting into the carriage hadn't been easy, either. At one point, the driver had gripped his arm to steady him, but still hadn't said anything.

That wasn't repeated here. With the help of his cane Logan managed to get both feet on the ground. He nodded to the driver and said, "Thank you."

The man just returned the nod silently.

Logan walked toward the entrance. He had shined his boots and brushed his hat. A diamond stickpin, one of the few relics of the old days, sparkled in his cravat. He knew he looked respectable enough that he shouldn't stand out in the crowd of the Baldwins' friends.

Respectable enough for a hired gun, anyway, he thought as a liveried footman swung the door open in front of him.

Inside, another servant took his hat, and yet another ushered him into a large ballroom lit by crystal chandeliers hanging from the ceiling. Logan had been in rooms like this before, but it had been a long time.

Quite a few people were on hand already, the men dressed in suits that put his to shame, the women glitteringly beautiful in their gowns and jewelry. Logan was standing there just inside the ballroom, leaning on his cane, when Gillian Baldwin spotted him, made her excuses to the people she was talking to, and came toward him with a dazzling smile on her face. She wore a light blue gown cut low enough to reveal the creamy upper swells of her breasts. The necklace around her throat probably cost more than he had earned some years.

"Logan!" she said. "You made it. I'm so glad you could come."

"I said I would," Logan pointed out.

"Of course." She linked her right arm with his left, which made him uncomfortable. The smooth, rounded warmth of her flesh ought to be pressed to a strong, vital arm, not a withered thing like his. That didn't seem to bother her, though, as she said, "Come along, I'll introduce you to some people."

Logan didn't really care who any of the other guests were, but he wanted to be polite to Gillian since he was going to be spending a considerable amount of time with her over the next few days. If he offended her it would just make things strained and awkward between them. So he smiled and nodded politely to everyone she introduced him to and even made a mostly unsuccessful effort to remember their names.

Marcus Baldwin came over. He had a drink in his left hand and used the right to shake hands with Logan again.

"So glad you could join us tonight, Mr. Handley," he said. "Here, I'd like for you to meet someone."

"I'm introducing Logan around, Father," Gillian said with a pout that Logan was sure got a lot of use in this house.

"This won't take but a moment." Baldwin turned and called, "Aaron."

A short, thick-bodied, bearded man turned toward them. He sauntered across the gleaming parquet floor and gave Baldwin a curt nod.

"Baldwin," he said in a gravelly voice. "Who's this?"

"Logan Handley," Baldwin said. "Logan, meet Aaron Nash. Aaron is my competition."

Baldwin chuckled, but there was no real humor in the sound.

"Heard about you," Nash said as he gripped Logan's right hand. "Just about everybody in this room owes you a debt of thanks for stopping those bank robbers. We all have money there."

"I didn't exactly stop them," Logan said. "I just spooked them enough to make them run outside the bank. Marshal Radcliffe and his deputies showed up just in time to take care of them from there."

Take care of them was a discreet way of saying that Radcliffe and his men had blown the bank robbers into bloody little pieces. But in this opulent room, with soft music being played by a string quartet in the corner, even thinking about such carnage seemed out of place.

"Well, it's good to know that someone was willing to stand up to those outlaws, anyway," Nash said. "And it's good to meet you, Handley."

He gave them another brusque nod and moved off into the crowd. Baldwin, still smiling, watched him go and said quietly, "I hate that son of a bitch. But no more than he hates me."

"He's another timber man?"

"That's right. He – "

Baldwin stopped short as another man approached them with a woman on his arm. The newcomer said, "Hello, Marcus. I saw you talking to Aaron just now."

He was about as tall as Logan, with bushy side whiskers and a full, luxuriantly brown mustache. Although Logan was no real judge of such things, he supposed the man was good-looking, probably too handsome to be with the rather plain woman beside him.

Her gown was expensive, but it didn't really flatter her since her body had little shape to it. Her hair was a mousy brown and was pulled back severely, and that did nothing to soften the angular lines of her face.

Logan thought she had nice brown eyes, though, and he saw both sadness and sweetness in them.

"Hello, Carleton," Baldwin said. He nodded to the woman. "Elizabeth."

She said, "You and Father aren't at each other's throats again, are you, Marcus?"

Baldwin laughed. "Oh, no, certainly not. Aaron and I have long since made peace, you know that. We're just friendly rivals."

The other man stuck his hand out to Logan and said, "Carleton Eastland, at your service, sir."

Logan's interest had perked up as soon as he heard Baldwin address the man as Carleton. He remembered that was the name of Vickie's former husband. Now that Eastland had introduced himself, there was no doubt of his identity.

Eastland leaned his head toward the woman and went on, "My darling wife Elizabeth."

Logan shook hands with Eastland and nodded to the woman. "Ma'am," he said. "It's a pleasure."

"This is Logan Handley," Baldwin said. "He's working for me now."

"Ah, the famous slayer of bank robbers," Eastland said.

Logan shook his head. "I didn't slay anybody."
Not here, anyway.

"Well, you helped stop them, at any rate, and that's quite impressive for a man with your, ah, limitations."

"I do what I can," Logan said. He resisted the temptation to add, *You pompous ass.*

So that was the man who divorced Vickie, he thought as the Eastlands drifted off into the crowd. He still didn't know the details of what had caused the split, but it seemed odd that Eastland would have turned around and married such a plain woman after having been married to Vickie. Logan knew there was no accounting for emotions, however. Maybe Eastland really loved her.

Then Baldwin put a stop to that line of thought by saying, "If there's anyone I despise more than Aaron Nash, it's his son-in-law."

"You mean Eastland? Elizabeth is Nash's daughter?"

"That's right. You've been staying at the boarding house Eastland's former wife runs, haven't you?"

"That's right."

Baldwin took a sip of his drink and said, "We'll have to do something about that. A man who works for me should have a place of his own. A better place. We'll talk about it when you get back from Little Rock."

"All right," Logan said. He had been thinking that he needed to move out of the boarding house, so that Vickie and Rusty and the other boarders would be safer, and with Baldwin's help he could probably afford to do that.

But a part of him felt a twinge of regret at the thought of leaving the friends he had made. He felt the same way about not working for Doc Reese and Dewey Dumont anymore.

He put that out of his mind as a soft, warm shape pressed against his side again.

"You've monopolized Logan long enough, Father," Gillian said. "I'm taking him over again."

"Of course, my dear," Baldwin said with an indulgent smile.

Gillian steered Logan away from her father and said, "I suppose dancing would be difficult for you, wouldn't it?"

"Impossible," Logan said.

"But there's nothing to stop us from watching the others." Gillian lowered her voice. "I can tell you all about them. I know all the gossip."

Logan didn't doubt it.

14.

Gillian led him to a comfortable divan in a small alcove where they could still see most of the ballroom. She sat down next to him and left her arm linked with his. He was aware of the yielding but insistent pressure of her breast against his arm.

After listening to her prattle for a few minutes about the people moving past them, Logan spotted Carleton and Elizabeth Eastland and said, "What about those two? They seem to be a rather odd couple."

"Aren't they, though?" Gillian said. "Carleton married her for her money, of course, and to secure a better position in her father's company. Aaron Nash couldn't very well leave his new son-in-law in the lowliest of clerical positions, now could he?"

"I suppose not. I'm acquainted with the former Mrs. Eastland – "

"Of course you are. You live in her boarding house, don't you? Victoria Eastland is much more attractive than that poor little mouse Elizabeth. Carleton definitely didn't get the better end of the bargain in that respect. But speaking of mice, it's a shame the woman has the morals of an alley cat."

"Elizabeth?"

Gillian laughed and shook her head. "Of course not. I was talking about the former Mrs. Eastland. It was her . . . indiscretion . . . with another man that led to Carleton divorcing her."

Logan frowned and said, "I find that hard to believe."

"You can believe it," Gillian assured him. "Carleton caught them together. All the sordid details came out in court. The man admitted what he and Mrs. Eastland had done, but of course what other choice did he have? He was lucky Carleton didn't put a bullet through his head."

What he had just heard seemed impossible to Logan. He couldn't imagine the cool, reserved Vickie Eastland he knew cheating on her husband. But maybe he didn't really know her all that well, he told himself. In all the weeks he had lived in the boarding house, they had never really had more than polite, perfunctory conversations.

To change the subject, he said, "I'd be honored to meet your mother."

Gillian stiffened beside him. She said, "My mother passed away years ago, Logan."

"Oh." He felt like an utter fool. He hurried on, "I'm sorry – "

She stopped him with a graceful motion of her hand. "Don't be. There's no way you could have known. It's just the two of us, Father and I. It's much the same with Elizabeth. Only children, she and I, and disappointments to our widower fathers because we weren't sons bred to take over the business. But what can you do other than make the best of what life has given you?"

"I understand that," Logan muttered.

"I'm sure you do. I can already tell that you and I are a lot alike, Logan. We're practical people. We do what we have to in order to get what we want."

Before he could think about whether she meant anything by that, Carleton Eastland walked up and said, "Gillian, my dear, can I steal you away from Mr. Handley for a dance?"

"Oh, I don't know – "

Logan told her, "Go ahead." He had seen the way she smiled and leaned forward slightly at Eastland's invitation. Gillian was the sort of woman who enjoyed attention, and there was nothing wrong with that as far as Logan was concerned.

"You're sure?" she said to him.

"I'll be fine," he said with a smile.

"All right, then." She stood up and took Eastland's arm. They whirled away to join the other dancing couples. Logan stayed on the divan, resting both hands on the head of his cane as it leaned on the floor in front of him.

Gillian and Eastland didn't dance just the one dance. She remained in his arms as the musicians began playing another waltz. Eastland was talking to her, and from time to time Gillian laughed merrily. Logan thought at first she was just being polite, but he began to think the laughter was genuine. Carleton Eastland was a handsome man. Gillian had to enjoy sweeping around the floor in his arms. The two of them looked like they were made for each other, Logan thought.

There was no reason for that to bother him, other than the instinctive dislike he felt for Eastland. And that was probably just because he knew Vickie and admired her.

Marcus Baldwin came over with two drinks, handed one of them to Logan, and sat down beside him.

"I'm not overly fond of these parties," he said. "Gillian seems to enjoy them, though. They give everyone a chance to tell her how beautiful and wonderful she is."

"That's what Carleton Eastland seems to be doing," Logan said.

"That pompous – " Baldwin stopped himself and downed some of his drink.

"I was thinking the same thing a little earlier."

"Eastland is annoying, but he's harmless. It's Nash who's the real threat. He's a ruthless monster." Baldwin looked over at Logan. "He's another reason I wanted you to work for me, Logan."

"I thought you were worried about bandits."

"I am, but Nash wouldn't be above hiring cutthroats to steal that payroll of mine. He'll do anything to cause trouble for me. The man's out to destroy me."

"Why would he want to do that?" Logan asked. "I know the two of you are business rivals – "

"It's more than that," Baldwin said harshly. His hand tightened on the thick-walled glass he held. "Several years ago Nash moved in a stretch of timber I thought I had in my pocket and snatched it right out from under me. I didn't take kindly to that."

Logan was willing to bet that he didn't.

"I had my freight line undercut the prices of all the other freight outfits around here," Baldwin went on. "When I had put them all out of business, Nash was forced to use my wagons if he wanted to get supplies in and timber out. He didn't like it a bit when I raised the prices, but he had no choice except to pay or buy his own wagons."

Logan realized now that he had stumbled into the same sort of situation in which he had found himself many times in the past: two rich, powerful men who hated each other and were willing to go to any lengths to hurt the other one, including hiring gunmen. Being paid to take a hand in such grudges had been Logan's way of making a living for years . . . but things were different now. If he had to go up against a professional – a healthy professional – chances were he would lose, even with that sawed-off double-barrel to help even the odds.

Maybe Baldwin had hired him just to guard that payroll and Gillian. Maybe the man didn't plan to use him to cause trouble for Aaron Nash. He could always back out, Logan told himself.

But he didn't want to. Gillian was right: they had to make the best of what life had given them. The only things of real value he possessed were his cool nerves and his ability to use a gun. Even if that ability was impaired, it was still something.

He was a gunman. It was time to stop denying that.

"You all right, Logan?" Baldwin asked. "You look rather preoccupied."

"I'm fine," Logan said. He looked across the ballroom. There was another alcove like this one on the other side, with a similar divan in it.

Elizabeth Eastland sat alone on that divan.

Logan looked at the dancing couples. Gillian had her head resting on Carleton Eastland's shoulder now. Logan looked at Elizabeth again and realized that she was watching Gillian and her husband, too.

He used the cane to push himself to his feet and said, "Excuse me, Mr. Baldwin." He threw back the rest of the brandy in his glass and handed the empty to Baldwin, who took it looking rather surprised. Then Logan began making his way around the room.

Elizabeth was still alone when he reached the other alcove. He smiled and said, "I can't ask you to dance, Mrs. Eastland, but I'd be honored if I could sit and talk with you for a few moments if you'd allow it."

She looked surprised, too, but after a second she nodded and said, "Of course, Mister . . . Handley, was it?"

"That's right. Logan Handley." He lowered himself on the divan beside her, keeping a discreet distance between them. "It's quite a party, isn't it?"

"Of course. Only the best for dear Gillian."

He heard the dislike in her voice and said, "You and Miss Baldwin don't get along? I gathered that the two of you were childhood friends or something like that."

Gillian hadn't actually said that or even implied it, but the two women were about the same age and Hot Springs wasn't a very big town, relatively speaking. Since their fathers were in the same business, it made sense that they would have known each other for quite a while.

"We were friends . . . or something like that, as you put it . . . at one time, but that all changed when Gillian realized that pretty girls can get anything they want just by smiling and batting their eyelashes."

The bitterness in her voice tempted Logan to point out that rich girls had a natural advantage in getting what they wanted, too, and Carleton Eastland was living proof of that. He was too polite to put that thought into words. Besides, Elizabeth's pain seemed genuine, and he could sympathize with that even though it was emotional and not physical.

Instead he said, "I've met your husband and your father. Is there anyone else here I should know?"

"Not really. They're all dull and pretentious." She smiled. "Like me."

"I don't find you the least bit dull," Logan said. "In fact, I'd like to hear all about you."

"Really?" She brightened momentarily but then shook her head. "You're just being polite."

"Not at all. Have you lived here in Hot Springs all your life?"

"Well . . . here and in various logging camps."

"That sounds exciting."

Elizabeth shook her head again and said, "It wasn't. It was just dreary and dirty. And in the summer, the heat and the mosquitoes . . ." She sighed. "I'm convinced it was all those hardships that weakened my mother until she fell ill and died."

"I'm sorry."

"Thank you. I miss her. The past few years would have been easier if she had still been around to help me. During the war everything was so dreadful. The Yankees came in and took over, you know. They were everywhere."

"Was your father aligned with the Confederacy? Did that cause trouble for him?"

"My father has always been aligned with whoever would buy his timber from him," Elizabeth said with a wry smile, "including the Yankees. He got along fine with them, just like Marcus Baldwin did. It's easier to get along in the world when your only objective is making money."

That was probably true, Logan thought. He had lived in the same way for the past decade. A mercenary attitude simplified life, if nothing else.

As long as you could quell the occasional stirrings of dissatisfaction, the nagging sense that there ought to be something more, that life ought to *amount* to something other than money in the bank . . .

He pushed those thoughts out of his head as Elizabeth asked him about some of the places he had lived and visited. Since he had been almost everywhere west of the Mississippi, from the Rio Grande to the Canadian border, he was able to regale her with several tales about places far away from the wooded hills of Arkansas . . . heavily edited, of course, to take out any mention of all the sordid violence that had accompanied his travels.

She hung on his every word and seemed to be enjoying herself. She probably didn't get that much male attention, Logan thought. From what he had seen tonight, Carleton Eastland had deserted her as soon as he got the opportunity.

After a while, during a lull in the conversation, Elizabeth asked, "I don't want to intrude, but how were you injured?"

Logan shook his head and said, "It wasn't an injury. I got sick, and it affected my nerves and muscles. For a long time I wasn't able to use my left arm or my right leg. I've been trying to strengthen them again, but it hasn't been easy."

"I'm sure it hasn't. That's such a shame."

"Indeed it is. If not for my affliction, I'd have you out there on the dance floor right now, Mrs. Eastland."

She laughed, and for the first time the sound struck him as genuine. Laying a hand on his arm, she said, "Oh, no, you wouldn't want that, Mr. Handley. I'm afraid I'm not very graceful. I'd be stepping on your toes all the time. You'd really limp by the time I was through with you." Her eyes widened abruptly. "Oh, dear. That was a terribly thoughtless thing to say – "

"Not at all," he told her, smiling. "And I'm sure you're much more graceful than you're giving yourself credit for."

She shook her head, and he realized that she had moved closer. Not as close as Gillian had been to him earlier, but almost.

"Thank you for sitting with me and being so nice," she said. "I'm afraid I've lost Carleton to Gillian for the rest of the evening – "

"No," Logan said as he caught sight of movement from the corner of his eye. "In fact, here he comes now."

It was true. Carleton Eastland was striding across the ballroom toward them.

And unless Logan was mistaken, the man's face was flushed with rage.

15.

"What's going on here?" Eastland demanded as he came to a stop in front of the divan where Logan and Elizabeth sat. Logan glanced past the man and saw Gillian Baldwin halfway across the ballroom, watching them. The smile on Gillian's face seemed to say that she was enjoying herself.

"Mr. Handley and I were just talking, dear – " Elizabeth began.

"It looked like more than that to me," Eastland snapped, interrupting her. "It looked like you were pawing him. A damned cripple!"

Logan leaned on his cane and pushed himself to his feet.

"I'll thank you to watch what you're saying, sir," he said. "You're not only insulting me, but you shouldn't speak to your wife in that manner."

"I'll speak to my wife in any manner that suits me," Eastland replied with a sneer. "And as for you, sir, I'll thank you to leave her alone. I can't take you outside and thrash you, not a man in your condition, but I promise you, if things were different – "

With anger burning inside him now, Logan leaned closer to Eastland and said in quiet, menacing tones, "Don't let that stop you. I can handle a man like you with one good arm and one good leg."

Contempt dripped from his words. He had killed men for being less obnoxious than Carleton Eastland was being now.

Eastland paled at the challenge. His hands clenched into fists. He took a step toward Logan.

Across the room, Gillian's smile widened in anticipation.

Marcus Baldwin suddenly appeared at Logan's side. He deftly insinuated himself between the two men.

"Here now, what's all this?" he said. "We don't need to make a scene, gentlemen. That would just ruin a perfectly good party."

Aaron Nash arrived at the confrontation, too, and clapped a hand on his son-in-law's shoulder.

"Come on, Carleton," he said in bluffy, hearty tones. "I think we could both use a drink, my boy."

Eastland said, "Tell your daughter – "

Nash's hand tightened on his shoulder and stopped him.

"You mean your wife. I gave her to you at the wedding, remember?"

Logan glanced at Elizabeth. Her face was pale and strained. Her brown eyes, her best feature, were cast toward the floor.

"How about that drink?" Nash prodded Eastland.

"I don't think I'm thirsty," Eastland said. He looked like he wanted to shake Nash's hand off his shoulder, but Logan knew Eastland was unlikely to forget, even under duress, that Nash was not only his father-in-law but also his employer. A rich, powerful employer, at that. Eastland took a deep breath, brought his anger under control with a visible effort, and went on, "I believe I'd like to leave. I've had enough of this party. Come along, Elizabeth."

She lifted her head, and with a display of defiance that surprised Logan, she asked, "What if I'm not ready to leave yet?"

Nash let go of Eastland and stepped over beside his daughter.

"I think Carleton's right," he said. "It might be best, my dear."

Elizabeth looked back and forth between her husband and her father for a moment, then sighed. She was willing to argue with one of them, thought Logan, but not both. That was beyond the limits of her stubbornness.

"All right," she murmured as she got to her feet. She started to turn toward Logan, perhaps to bid him a good night.

Carleton Eastland caught hold of her arm and stopped her. He said curtly, "Come on," and started toward the entrance. Elizabeth had no choice but to go with him, but she cast a last glance over her shoulder at Logan.

Baldwin stood there beside him, watching as Nash, Eastland, and Elizabeth made their way across the ballroom. Quietly, Baldwin said, "You see the sort of man Nash attracts to his business. He's an utter scoundrel, Eastland is, which makes him a good match for Aaron Nash."

"Your daughter told me that Eastland divorced his first wife because she was unfaithful to him," Logan said. "Is there any truth to that rumor?"

Baldwin frowned and said, "It's not a rumor. The first Mrs. Eastland was involved with a man named Jonas Hulsey. Eastland caught them . . . together, you know."

Baldwin cocked his head to the side and raised his eyebrows suggestively.

"Now, personally, I thought the way he handled the matter was rather cowardly," he went on. "A real man, faced with such a situation, would have taken out a pistol and shot Hulsey. Eastland would have been perfectly within his rights to do so, and no one would have objected. He probably could have shot Mrs. Eastland, too, and gotten away with it, but that would have been almost too sordid. I think a good beating would have sufficed."

The thought of Vickie being beaten by a man like Carleton Eastland made Logan's hands tighten angrily on the head of his cane.

Baldwin might have noticed that reaction, because he went on, "In principle, of course. Personally, from what little I know of the woman, Victoria Eastland was always a good wife to him until that one indiscretion. Better than what an arrogant, self-important jackass like Carleton Eastland deserves, certainly."

Logan certainly couldn't argue with that.

"Anyway," Baldwin continued, "you should be very careful on your way to Little Rock with my daughter and that payroll. Not all the men Aaron Nash hires are as incompetent as Carleton Eastland."

"Surely he wouldn't do anything to harm Miss Baldwin," Logan said.

"To tell you the truth, Logan . . . I wouldn't put anything past that man."

* * *

The lamp in the study was turned low, but it was still bright enough to cast its glow over the papers spread out on the desk in front of Aaron Nash. The short, burly, bearded man had taken off his coat and cravat and rolled up the sleeves of his shirt over muscular, hairy forearms, but other than that he was dressed the same as he had been at the party earlier in the evening.

The hour was late, and most men would have turned in by now. Carleton Eastland, who lived here in Nash's mansion along with his wife, certainly had. Eastland had gone straight to his room once the three of them were in the house. He no longer shared a room with Elizabeth and hadn't for months. Nash didn't think about such things. Being the father of an unattractive daughter, he had never held out much hope for grandchildren in the first place, so it didn't really matter that Eastland and Elizabeth slept apart.

Anyway, grandchildren might have been nice . . . someone to leave his company to someday . . . but destroying Marcus Baldwin would be better. And *that* was something Nash fully intended to do.

His pen scratched as he made notes on the reports from his subordinates he was reading. First thing in the morning, he would turn the papers over to Eastland, whose job it would be to see that Nash's orders in these matters were carried out. Eastland might be the vice-president of the Nash Timber Company now, but he was still just a glorified clerk and that was all he would ever be.

The atmosphere in the carriage during the ride back from Baldwin's mansion had been very tense. Eastland was still furious with jealousy, which was ludicrous and unfair since he'd been fawning all over the Baldwin girl. Nash supposed it was good to see evidence of *some* feeling for his daughter on Eastland's part. Even a bought-and-paid-for husband ought to try to have a *little* affection for his wife. Nash didn't interject himself into the dispute, though. He just sat and smoked a cigar in silence. When they'd reached the house, he had poured himself a brandy, gone to his room briefly to get rid of his coat and tie, and then stomped into the study to get a little work done.

No point in the whole evening going to waste.

He scribbled another order on one of the reports and was pushing it aside when he heard the French door that opened out onto a balcony swing back into the room. He looked up as a dark figure slouched in from the balcony and then stopped to remain in the shadows beyond the reach of the lamp's pale glow.

Nash was pretty sure he knew his visitor's identity, but his hand strayed toward an open desk drawer beside him where a Smith & Wesson .32 caliber revolver lay within easy reach.

Before he could grasp the gun, the man in the shadows drawled, "Was it Handley?"

Nash relaxed. He had been right about the man's identity.

"Yes," he said. "Logan Handley, the former gunman. The once and future gunman, I should say, since the rumor is that Baldwin has hired him to protect that payroll on its way to Little Rock tomorrow." A harsh laugh came from Nash's mouth. "Further proof, as if we needed it, that Marcus Baldwin is a fool. Just like you heard, Handley has been crippled by some sort of disease. He can get around with the help of a cane, but his left arm appears to be all but useless."

"His gun arm," the visitor mused.

"He certainly doesn't seem to have lost any of his fiery temper, though," Nash went on. "He was quick enough to challenge that oaf of a son-in-law of mine when Carleton confronted him."

The man in the shadows asked, "What led Eastland to have a run-in with Handley?"

Nash explained about Eastland's jealous reaction to the sight of Handley sitting and talking with Elizabeth. The whole thing sounded even more ridiculous to his ears when he put it into words.

"Handley was ready to fight when Carleton called him a cripple," Nash concluded. "He would have done it, too. I could tell by the look in his eyes."

That drew a chuckle from the other man, who said, "Logan never did take to insults. He was really too thin-skinned for our line of work." He changed the subject abruptly by asking, "You still want me to hit that train and try to get Baldwin's payroll?"

Nash considered the question for a long moment before he shook his head.

"No, let's let things calm down for a while. That'll get Baldwin off his guard. I want to see if he keeps Handley on anyway."

"I hope he does." A match scraped and flared to life. The man in the shadows lifted the flame to light the cigarette he had rolled and put between his lips. The glare revealed a lean, wolfish face that would have been handsome if not for the ugly scar that stretched across the right cheek all the way back to the ear, part of which was missing, shot off by the same bullet that had plowed the groove in the side of the man's face. The scar made the skin pull at a grotesque angle as Jim Meadows smiled and added, "Logan Handley and I have a few scores to settle."

16.

Rusty went with Logan to the train station the next morning, carrying the carpetbag and the wooden case they had picked up at Buck Finnerty's shop containing the sawed-off shotgun. Logan's coat covered the butt of the short-barreled Colt he carried in a cross-draw rig on his left hip where he could reach it easily with his right hand.

The holster Finnerty had fashioned for the shotgun was packed away in the carpetbag for the moment. Even though the sawed-off with its pistol grip was short, it couldn't be carried holstered without being out in the open where it was visible. Logan thought it might be better if it wasn't so obvious that he was armed.

"You won't get in trouble for not being at work at the freight company this morning, will you?" Logan asked his friend as they neared the depot.

"Hey, I'm helpin' you, and you work for Mr. Baldwin now, too, so I figure I *am* at work, in a manner of speakin'."

Logan laughed and said, "I hope Mr. Baldwin follows that same line of reasoning."

A carriage stopped in front of the station just as Logan and Rusty got there. Logan recognized it as the same one that had picked him up at the boarding house the previous night. The taciturn driver was the same, too. So he wasn't surprised when the man opened the door and Marcus Baldwin climbed out of the vehicle, followed by Gillian, who was resplendent in a bottle green traveling outfit and hat.

She smiled and said, "Logan, there you are. Perfect timing, as always."

Baldwin nodded a greeting to Logan, then said to Gillian, "I'll see you on board the train, my dear, and then I need to have a talk with Mr. Handley before the two of you leave."

"Of course, Father."

Baldwin glanced at Logan. "Wait for me in the depot."

Logan nodded. Baldwin seemed brusque and distracted this morning, but he was probably a little worried. He had valuable freight headed for Little Rock on this train: his daughter and his money.

Logan and Rusty went into the station. Logan sat down on one of the benches in the waiting room. Rusty placed the two bags beside him.

"Are you sure you can manage from here?" the older man asked.

"Yes, if I need help, there are porters around."

"Well, then, all right." Rusty shook hands with him and added, "Good luck on your trip. You be careful."

"With Mr. Baldwin's payroll, you mean."

"And with that gal," Rusty said.

"I don't intend to let anything happen to her."

Rusty squinted and said, "That ain't *exactly* what I was talkin' about. Miss Gillian, she's as pretty as any gal in the state and she can be mighty nice when she wants to, but she can be a mite headstrong, too. From what I've heard, her pa's had his hands full ridin' herd on her sometimes."

"I'll keep that in mind," Logan said with a nod. He wasn't surprised to hear that Gillian had caused trouble for her father. He had already figured out that she was self-centered, willful, and accustomed to getting her own way, as almost any young woman that beautiful would be.

Rusty left the depot, and a few minutes later Marcus Baldwin returned.

"I've got Gillian settled in my private car," he told Logan. "You'll be traveling there, too, of course. That's where the payroll is. The safe in there is stronger than the one in the express car."

"Am I supposed to deliver it to someone in Little Rock?" Logan asked.

Baldwin shook his head. "No, one of my employees, accompanied by a group of armed guards, will meet the train and collect the payroll. He knows the safe's combination. They'll take the money to the mill. Once they've picked it up, that part of the job is over for you. The easy part, I should say. You'll still have to keep up with Gillian."

"I think I can manage," Logan said.

"I hope you're right. The two of you will be staying in my usual suite in a hotel down there." Baldwin frowned. "I expect that you'll comport yourself as a gentleman the entire time. I thought about sending one of the maids from the house here along with you as a chaperone, but Gillian wouldn't hear of it."

"My only interest in your daughter is in keeping her safe, sir."

Baldwin grunted. "And in earning that three hundred dollars, eh?"

"I hope to begin treatments soon with Dr. August Strittmatter," Logan said. He hadn't mentioned that specifically to Baldwin before.

"Strittmatter! He's supposed to be a good man. Although he is a damned foreigner, of course. But a lot of people say that he and his mineral baths have worked wonders for him."

"I could use having a few wonders worked," Logan said.

"Yes, no doubt." Baldwin became businesslike again as he went on, "You're clear on everything?"

"I think so."

"You'll return to Hot Springs whenever Gillian is ready. Arrangements are already made with the railroad. My car will remain on the siding down there until you have need of it again." Baldwin held out his hand and said the same thing Rusty had a few minutes earlier. "Good luck."

"I don't intend to need it," Logan said with a smile as he gripped Baldwin's hand.

* * *

A porter carried Logan's bag and the shotgun case and showed him to the private car belonging to Marcus Baldwin. Logan wasn't a bit surprised that Baldwin had his own train car. A man so rich couldn't be expected to ride with the common people in the regular coaches.

The car had a carpeted sitting room furnished with comfortable, heavy furniture. The windows had actual curtains hanging in front of them instead of plain shades. There was even a bar with a number of bottles of whiskey, brandy, and port in a cabinet behind it.

A door at the far end of the sitting room led to a pair of bedrooms. The accommodations wouldn't be needed for this trip, since Little Rock was only about fifty miles away and the train would be there by early afternoon.

"Where would you like these, sir?" the porter asked, hefting the carpetbag and the wooden case.

"You can set the bag down there in the corner, out of the way." Logan thought for a second. "Put the case on the bar."

He wanted to have the scattergun handy.

Logan gave the man a half-dollar, then went over to one of the windows to watch the people coming and going on the station platform. It never hurt to keep an eye on such activity. A fellow never knew when he might see something important.

The crowd on the platform this morning seemed utterly harmless, though: mostly men in tweed suits and bowler hats or derbies traveling on business and women with children probably going to visit relatives.

His eyes suddenly narrowed as he caught sight of a man walking through the depot's waiting room. It was only a glimpse, and the man's back was to Logan, but there was something familiar about him . . .

Logan shook his head. The odds of him knowing anyone here in Hot Springs other than the folks he had met since coming to town were so small as to be insignificant. Just because the briefly seen man reminded him of someone didn't mean anything.

He heard the door open behind him and turned away from the window. Gillian emerged from the rooms at the other end of the car. She had taken off her hat but was still dressed for traveling otherwise.

"I hope the train leaves soon," she said. "I hate waiting."

"I've had to learn to be patient."

"Yes, I suppose you would, in your line of work. You've probably had to lie in wait for men so you could ambush them."

He stiffened. She had spoken carelessly, as if she gave no thought to what she was saying and meant no offense, but he didn't like it anyway.

"I've run into plenty of backshooters," he said, "but I've never been one myself."

"Oh." She looked a little surprised. "I've said something I shouldn't have. I didn't mean to insult you, Logan. I just assumed that such things were part of your work. You were hired to kill men, weren't you?"

"I was." He didn't see any point in denying it or trying to make it something less than it was. "But that didn't keep me from killing them face to face, with them having the same chance as me."

That wasn't strictly true. Some of the men he'd squared off against hadn't been in the same class as him when it came to handling a gun, and he had known it at the time and faced them anyway. But at least every man he'd killed had taken his lead from the front, and they had died with guns in their own hands, too.

"Well, I'm sorry," Gillian said. "I don't really know much about that sort of thing. You and I, we've spent our lives almost in different worlds, wouldn't you say?"

That brought a faint smile to Logan's face. "I think I've spent more time in your world than you have in mine."

"And thank goodness for that!" she said with a laugh. "I don't think I'd make a very good gunfighter, do you?"

"Oh, I don't know," he said, still smiling. "I think you're icy-nerved enough that you might could get by."

"And ruthless," she said. "Don't forget ruthless. I get what I want."

"Sounds like the makings of a pistoleer," Logan said.

The train's whistle blew, a shrill shriek that reached from cowcatcher to caboose, and a second later with a hiss of steam, a cloud of smoke from the diamond-shaped stack, and the clatter of the drivers on the steel rails, the locomotive lurched into motion and rolled out of Hot Springs.

17.

Logan and Gillian spent the first part of the trip lounging in overstuffed chairs in the private car, chatting idly as the thickly wooded hills rolled past outside the windows. It was a beautiful sunny day, on the cool side but not unpleasant.

Gillian made a few veiled comments about having some wine, but Logan pretended not to hear them. It was too early in the day for drinking, for one thing, and for another he was well aware of the squat, massive safe sitting in one corner of the room. With the double responsibility he had today, he knew it would be better if he kept a clear head. He might well maintain that resolve for the entire journey, he thought. Even with everything he had suffered, he wasn't the sort to retreat into a bottle.

He wasn't really paying that much attention to what Gillian was saying, but he sat up straighter when he heard Vickie Eastland's name. He said, "I'm sorry, what was that?"

"I just asked if you said anything to Mrs. Eastland about what I told you last night."

Logan shook his head. "No, I didn't. Why would I?"

"I thought you might have asked her if it was true. I could tell when we were talking about it that you didn't believe me. Or that you didn't want to believe me, anyway."

"I didn't mention it." As a matter of fact, Logan had barely seen Vickie since the previous evening. She had already gone to bed by the time the Baldwin carriage brought him back from the party, or at least she hadn't been downstairs. And this morning she had been busy and had seemed in no mood to talk. Logan respected that.

He didn't tell Gillian that her father had also mentioned the reason Carleton Eastland had divorced Vickie. Her affair with Jonas Hulsey, whoever he was, seemed to be common knowledge in Hot Springs, so Logan didn't see any point in stubbornly disbelieving the story.

"It's good that you didn't say anything. That might have been awkward, what with you living under her roof and all."

"Do you know her?" Logan asked.

"We've met. And I know plenty about her, of course. But I can't say that I know her well at all. She's older than me. She's twenty-nine. Almost thirty! She didn't grow up around here, either. I believe she's from somewhere up north. Ohio, maybe, or Pennsylvania. She came here when her husband went to work for Aaron Nash. They saved up and bought the boarding house, but then . . . well, you know what happened then. Carleton Eastland is still working for Aaron Nash, but the situation is hardly the same, is it?"

"Hardly," Logan agreed.

For someone who claimed to be barely acquainted with Vickie, Gillian seemed to know a lot about her. But Hot Springs was a relatively small town, Logan reminded himself. Most people around here probably knew quite a bit about their neighbors. It was difficult to blend in and not be noticed unless a person lived in a big city.

Nobody other than his doctors had really known him in Denver and Kansas City. He had been just one more face in the crowd, albeit a little more pathetic than some.

"I'm tired of talking about the Eastlands," Gillian said. "Tell me more about yourself."

Logan smiled and said, "It's not a particularly interesting story. What do you want to know?"

She leaned forward slightly in her chair and asked, "How many men have you killed?"

The question took Logan by surprise. The smile dropped off his face. He said, "I don't think that's a proper subject for me to discuss with a young lady – "

"I'm not a proper young lady." She laughed. "Well, I can be when I want to, but right now I'm not. You're the first real gunfighter I've ever met, Logan Handley. You may well be the only real gunfighter I ever meet. I want to know what it's like."

How could he explain something like that? The isolation, the fear he saw on the faces of nearly everyone he met, the fear he himself experienced because he had known that sooner or later he would meet a man who was faster on the draw and a better shot than he was. That combination was deadly.

Of course, now there were a lot of men who were faster than he was, and better shots, to boot. He could handle a gun right-handed better than an average man, but against a professional shootist it wouldn't even be close.

How could he explain to Gillian that in all likelihood his days were numbered no matter what he did? How could she understand that he was just trying to live out however much time he had left with his head held up, with some dignity instead of defeat?

He didn't have to explain anything. The brakes suddenly screamed, and both Logan and Gillian were almost pitched out of their chairs as the train began to shudder to a halt.

Logan caught himself with his good arm. His cane had fallen to the floor. He bent over and picked it up, pushed himself to his feet. He knew this wasn't a scheduled stop, because there weren't any between Hot Springs and Little Rock. Nor had they reached the state capital; there hadn't been time for that since the train left Hot Springs. And it wasn't a flag stop because the engineer would have seen the signal earlier and wouldn't have had to apply the brakes so hard.

That left only one possibility.

Somebody was forcing the train to stop, and that meant a holdup.

"What is it?" Gillian asked anxiously. "Is something wrong, Logan?"

He didn't answer her. Instead he turned and limped to the bar. He wasn't after a drink, though. The wooden case still lay on the bar, although it had slid a little on the hardwood when the train began slowing down so abruptly.

Logan unfastened the two latches and raised the case's lid. He reached inside with his right hand and grasped the shotgun's stock. He lifted it from the velvet bed around it and used his thumb to push aside the lever that allowed the barrels to break open. He took hold of the barrels with his left hand and pushed them down, causing the breech to swing open. The effort required to do that was enough to make a couple of beads of sweat pop out on his forehead, too.

Shotgun shells nestled in a row of holes along the bottom of the case. Still using his left hand, Logan picked up two of them and slid them into the empty barrels. When they were seated properly, he rested the underside of the barrels against the bar and used it to lever them back into position.

The shotgun snapped closed just as someone kicked open the door into the private car and Gillian screamed.

Logan turned and thrust out the shotgun at the end of his arm. His elbow was bent slightly so that it could give a little and not wind up sprained by the recoil if he had to fire the sawed-off shotgun. He held the gun out far enough, though, that it wouldn't come back into his face when it kicked, either. It was a professional's stance, instinctive now after years of practice and experience.

Two men in long dusters had rushed into the private car, but they stopped short as they found themselves looking down the twin black bores of those barrels. Logan kept his attention focused on them, but he was aware that several more men crowded onto the platform at the rear of the car.

The dusters, the bandannas, the pulled-down hats . . . Logan had seen it all before in recent weeks. These men weren't inexperienced, would-be desperadoes like the ones who had tried to rob the bank in Hot Springs, though. Logan looked into their eyes over the scattergun's barrels and knew that he had met these two men before.

"Hello, Jesse," he said.

The man in the lead frowned under the lowered brim of his hat.

"Do I know you, friend?" he asked. "Have we met?"

"A while back on another train," Logan said. "Brother Frank there collected a toll from me, along with all the other passengers."

Jesse James laughed. "You can't expect me to remember everybody we rob, amigo," he said. "Now why don't you put down that ol' sawed-off and nobody has to get hurt?"

Gillian stood to one side. Her eyes were wide with terror, and her breasts heaved as she breathed hard. Logan didn't know if that reaction was from fear or excitement or some of both.

His brain worked quickly. The outlaws probably weren't after Marcus Baldwin's payroll; it was doubtful that they even knew it was being shipped to Little Rock today, unless they had a spy in Baldwin's company who had tipped them off. Logan couldn't disregard that possibility, but he considered it unlikely. It was more probable that this was just another train robbery to the James brothers. They were out for whatever they could get.

"Look, there's nothing here for you but trouble," Logan said. "Just back out of here and go on about your business, and the buckshot in this scattergun can stay where it is."

Frank nudged his brother and said, "Safe back yonder in the corner. Some blasting powder might blow it open, if we can't convince this fancy-dressed peckerwood to use the combination."

"That'd be a good trick," said Logan, "considering that I don't know it."

"He's lying," Frank said.

Gillian spoke up. "No, he's not. This is my father's private car, and *I* don't have any idea what the combination to the safe is. But it doesn't matter. The thing's empty. I'm just going on an excursion to Little Rock, that's all."

One of the men on the platform, young by the sound of his voice, said, "She's a rich man's daughter, Jesse. Man's got to be rich to have his own personal railroad car, all fancy like this. We should take her with us, make the ol' buzzard pay to get her back safe and sound."

"Shut up," Jesse snapped. "We rob banks and trains, and even that wasn't our idea in the first place. We were driven to it, like Cole always says. We're not kidnappers." He turned his attention back to Logan and wiggled the revolver he held. "You got two barrels in that thing, mister. There are too many of us for you to put us all down, even with something like that."

"Maybe," Logan said. "But I can make sure that you don't live to see what happens."

For a long moment, the two cold stares met. Then Jesse James laughed and said, "You've got plenty of nerve, I'll give you that. Frank, back out of here. We're gonna leave these fine folks alone."

Even from the narrow strip of Frank James' face that Logan could see, he could tell that the outlaw wanted to argue with his brother. But Jesse gave the orders here, and after a couple of seconds Frank grunted and began to back toward the door. Jesse followed him. Neither outlaw holstered his gun.

"So this is the second time we've met," Jesse said to Logan. "I came out on top the first time, and this time you did. What do you think's gonna happen the *third* time our trails cross?"

"I don't know," Logan said. "But I expect it'll be a sight to see."

That brought a laugh from Jesse. He said, "I expect you're right," then turned to order his men, "Let's go. The other boys ought to be done cleaning out the express car by now."

Several men jumped down from the platform at the rear of the car. Jesse paused in the open doorway, raised his free hand to the brim of his hat, and said to Gillian, "Good day, ma'am." He disappeared from view as well.

Logan didn't start to lower the shotgun until the platform was clear. Even then he was still wary.

It was a good thing, because he had just started to turn away when one of the duster-clad men suddenly leaped onto the platform again, yelled, "I'll get the bastard for you, Jesse!" and lunged into the car with his gun pointed at Logan, ready to fire.

18.

In that frozen instant of time, Logan's instincts took over completely. He twisted toward the outlaw, and the shotgun came up fast. Flame blossomed from its right-hand barrel, accompanied by a boom that in the tight confines of the railroad car slammed against the ears like a giant fist.

The load of buckshot spread out just enough that it filled the duster-clad man's chest from one side to the other as it shredded flesh and pulped bone. The impact jolted the outlaw back as he pulled the trigger. The bullet from his six-gun thudded harmlessly into the car's ceiling. He caught his balance and stood there staring with bulging eyes, but only for a second. Then he fell over backward and landed in a limp sprawl that signified death.

Logan barked, "Get down!" at Gillian as several other members of the gang leaped back onto the platform and started to rush into the car, bristling with guns. He didn't know if she could hear him or not after the shotgun's thunderous blast. Logan was about to touch off the second barrel into the gang when through the ringing in his own ears he heard Jesse James yelling, "Hold it! Hold your fire, damn it!"

The outlaws hesitated, and so did Logan. He still had the shotgun leveled at them and only the slightest pressure would be needed on the trigger to fire the second blast.

Jesse bulled his way past the men and motioned for them to back off. His gun was holstered, and he told Logan, "Take it easy, friend. No need for any more shooting."

"But Jesse!" one of the gang objected. "He killed Pete!"

"Pete was a hotheaded young fool," Jesse snapped. "I'd already given the order to pull out. He shouldn't have taken it on himself to throw down on this fella."

"I'm glad you see it that way," Logan said. "I didn't want any killing."

He glanced over at Gillian, who had collapsed on a leather settee and clapped her hands over her ears. She huddled there looking terrified, ready to flinch if more shots rang out. He wanted to tell her it was all right . . . but he didn't know for sure yet if that was true.

"So we're not going to do anything about Pete?" one of the outlaws asked. Logan thought from the voice that the man was Frank James.

"We'll take him and see that he's laid to rest properly," Jesse said. "And maybe the rest of you will remember not to go against my orders in the future."

There was quite a bit of grumbling among the members of the gang, but several of them holstered their guns and picked up the dead man's body to carry it off the train.

Jesse James was the last one off the platform this time. He looked back through the open door at Logan and said, "Just a word of advice, friend. Might be a good idea if you and I didn't cross trails again."

"I'll bear that in mind," Logan said, "but I can't guarantee what fate might take it in its head to do."

"Don't reckon any of us can," Jesse James said. He lifted a hand in a salute of farewell, then was gone.

Logan waited until he heard the swift rataplan of

hoofbeats from outside and knew the outlaws were riding away. Then he lowered the scattergun. He placed it on the bar and went to the settee where Gillian still waited, trembling. Her eyes were pressed tightly closed.

He sat down beside her and put a hand on her arm. Her eyes flew open and she gasped. Her head jerked from side to side as she looked around the car.

"They're . . . they're gone?" she asked.

Logan nodded and said, "They're gone."

The only sign that the outlaws had been there was a large smear of blood on the floor, but he didn't point that out.

Gillian leaned toward him and threw her arms around his neck. She hugged him and pressed herself close. He felt the little shudders that went through her.

"I was so scared," she whispered. "I thought they were going to kill us. That was Jesse James!"

"I know," Logan said.

"We're lucky to be alive!"

"More than likely," he agreed.

She took him by surprise then, lifting her face to his and kissing him. The soft, warm, insistent pressure of her lips and the feel of her body against his sent a shiver through him. He was as human as the next man, and he responded to her even though he knew she didn't mean anything by what she was doing. She was just scared because of the violence that had come so close to her.

After a moment she pulled back and looked away from him. "Logan," she said, "Mr. Handley . . . I'm so sorry . . ."

"Don't be," he said. "We're alive, and that's the main thing. Believe me, I've come close enough to dying, often enough, to know that."

"I'm sure you have. I . . . I never saw anyone move like that. My eyes couldn't even follow you."

To Logan it had seemed that his reaction was almost painfully slow. He never should have let that outlaw get back in the railroad car to start with. And his shot had beaten the young man's only by a split-second. That had been enough time to save his life, but it was a lot closer than it should have been.

He suspected Gillian wouldn't understand that even if he tried to explain it to her, and at that moment he heard agitated voices approaching outside. He stood up and quickly moved over to the bar. The scattergun still had one loaded barrel if he needed to use it.

He didn't. The conductor and engineer climbed up onto the platform. The blue-uniformed conductor said, "Miss Baldwin, are you all right?"

Of course they were worried about Gillian, Logan thought; none of them wanted to have an important man like Marcus Baldwin angry at them.

Gillian stood up. She was in control of herself again, cool and calm as she said, "Of course I'm all right. Mr. Handley protected me from those terrible men."

"One of the brakemen said he heard some shots from in here." The conductor looked down at the blood on the floor. "What happened?"

"I was forced to shoot one of the outlaws," Logan said.

The engineer asked, "Did he get away?"

Logan shook his head. "No. His friends took his body with them when they rode off."

Both men stared at him. The conductor said, "And they didn't shoot you?"

"That was the James gang," Gillian said before Logan could answer. "Jesse James himself was in here. He ordered his men not to harm Mr. Handley."

"Why would he do that?" the conductor asked. The

man's eyes suddenly narrowed with suspicion. "Are you and Jesse James friends, mister?"

"Not at all," Logan said. "But he had decided not to rob us, and the man I had to kill went against those orders. He didn't like that, so he and his men took the body and rode off."

The engineer grunted and said, "Not before bendin' a gun barrel over my fireman's head when he tried to jump 'em."

"Not before cleaning out the other passengers and the express car, too," added the conductor. "You folks are lucky."

Logan wasn't sure if the conductor believed him, or if the man still suspected there was some sort of connection between him and Jesse James. If that was the case, there was nothing he could do about it, so he decided not to let it bother him.

Instead he said, "Will we be heading on to Little Rock soon?"

The conductor nodded. "Yeah, the track is clear. A couple of 'em jumped from a cutbank down onto the coal tender, climbed into the cab, and forced Roy to stop. Then the rest came out of the trees on horseback. The varmints are good at what they do, I'll give 'em that."

The conductor and engineer went back to their duties, and a few minutes later the train began to move again, rolling toward Little Rock. Gillian didn't say anything else about the kiss she and Logan had shared, and he didn't bring it up, either.

He already had enough complications in his life without adding to them.

* * *

Marcus Baldwin's man was waiting at the depot in Little Rock, and as soon as the train had stopped, he came aboard the private car followed by half a dozen heavily armed guards. Several local police officers were with him, too. Baldwin obviously had a lot of influence even here in the state capital.

The leader of the group, a tall, bearded man named Hanratty, showed Logan a letter from Baldwin authorizing him to take charge of the payroll. Gillian was acquainted with Hanratty, too, and also verified the man's identity for Logan. In a matter of minutes, Hanratty worked the combination on the safe, swung the heavy door open, and removed two valises from it.

Logan wasn't sorry to see the money go. He had carried out this part of the job successfully.

Now all he had to worry about was Gillian.

They went to the hotel where they would be staying and checked in, then enjoyed a late lunch while porters from the train station delivered Gillian's numerous pieces of luggage. Having sometimes lived out of saddlebags for weeks at a time, Logan was amused by how much the young woman had brought with her to spend one night away from home. She didn't travel light, that was for sure.

After they had eaten, Gillian went back up to the suite to put her hat on again before setting out on her shopping expedition. Logan went with her, of course. He didn't intend to let her out of his sight more than necessary until they got back to Hot Springs.

"You don't have to go with me," she told him. "I'm just going to several different dress shops and milliners. You'd be terribly bored, Logan."

"Your father is paying me to look after you," he said. "I intend to do my job."

"So that's the only reason you'd want to spend time with me? Because you're being paid to do it?"

He could tell by the smile on her face that she was joking, but she seemed genuinely interested in the answer to the question, too. He said, "Of course not. Any man in his right mind would be very happy to spend time with you."

"In that case, I suppose you can come with me after all."

He planned to whether she gave her permission or not, but he was just as glad he didn't have to fight with her over it.

She was right about one thing, though: he was bored. He sat off to the side in the shops, usually in an uncomfortable straight-backed chair, and watched while Gillian went through what seemed like every piece of clothing, every hat, every scarf and handkerchief, every bag, in each place. He didn't see the appeal of it, himself, but people had their own interests, he supposed.

The important thing was that she was safe, and when they got back to the hotel that evening, she told him at supper that they would be returning to Hot Springs the next day.

"I was talking to one of my old friends today, Priscilla Danton," Gillian said. "She was Madame Frederique's, remember?"

All the stores blended together in Logan's mind, and since Gillian had seemed to know someone at every one of them, what she said didn't do much to jog his memory. But he nodded and said, "Of course."

"She told me about an interesting place called Michael's that I ought to visit. They have dancing there, Priscilla said, and gambling as well."

"Sounds like a saloon," Logan said with a smile.

"Oh, no, it caters to a much better class of people than a mere saloon. It's in one of the fine old houses here and is run by a true gentleman. I'd like to go."

Logan tilted his head to the side and said, "I don't know . . . It doesn't really sound like the sort of place your father would like for you to visit."

"Well, my father's not here, is he?" Gillian snapped. "And I don't know if you've noticed or not, Logan, but I'm a grown woman."

Oh, he had noticed, he thought. He had noticed plenty.

"Of course," she went on, her attitude changing abruptly, "if you'd rather stay in the suite this evening, I'm sure we could think of something to do. I was so impressed by your bravery today, and you were so gallant to defend me and then comfort me when the danger was over . . . I'd certainly like to repay you for all the kindness you've shown me, Logan."

The look in her eyes made it clear that expressing her gratitude could take whatever form he wanted it to. He was tempted, but only for a brief moment. He reminded himself again that he didn't need any extra complications in his life and said, "I don't think that would be a good idea, either. It's been a long day for both of us. I think we should make an early night of it."

Each in their own room in the suite, he thought. He hoped he wouldn't have to spell that out to Gillian. It would be awkward if he did.

She tried pouting, but it didn't work on him. After a few minutes she said, "All right. I suppose I *am* pretty tired, and it's probably a good idea to get a good night's sleep before that long train ride tomorrow. But if you change your mind . . . you'll know where to find me."

Logan wasn't going to change his mind. He had more sense than that.

At least he hoped he did.

19.

When they were back in the suite, Gillian said good night and vanished into her room. Logan had no reason to stay up and did the same.

He was getting ready for bed and had his shirt off when he heard a noise in the sitting room. Thinking that Gillian might need something, he sighed and pulled his shirt back on, fastening the buttons awkwardly as he went to the door. He opened it and looked into the sitting room.

Before leaving the room earlier, he had blown out the lamps. They were still out, and the room was dark. Enough light came from his bedroom for him to be able to make out the shapes of the furniture, but that was all. He didn't hear anyone moving around.

Yet he would have sworn that he had, a moment earlier, he thought as a frown creased his forehead. Actually, the noise he'd heard had sounded like someone bumping into a piece of furniture in the dark.

"Is anyone there?" he called softly. "Miss Baldwin?"

The rest of the suite was silent now.

Logan stepped over to the dressing table where he had placed the holstered Colt and slid the short-barreled revolver from leather. He returned to the door between the bedroom and sitting room and went through it as quickly as he could so he wouldn't be silhouetted against the light from the bedroom lamp for more than a moment. He went to the door of Gillian's room and rapped on it with the butt of his gun.

"Miss Baldwin? Gillian?"

Still no answer. Logan bit back a curse. If she was playing some sort of trick on him, or trying to lure him into her bedroom so she could seduce him, he was going to feel foolish. But so was she, when she found out it wasn't going to work.

But even if that was what he was dealing with here, he had to be sure she was all right. He had to know where she was.

He grasped the knob with his left hand. It wasn't very strong, but he could turn a doorknob with it.

As he did, he nudged the door open with his right foot. The room beyond was dark. Again, some of the light from his room reached it, but only enough for him to make out where the bed was, not whether anyone was in it. He limped closer and said, "Miss Baldwin, this needs to stop – "

He saw now the lightness of rumpled sheets, but no dark patch of a body lying on them. He reached down with his left hand and ran his palm over the sheets. They were cool and empty.

Gillian wasn't here.

Logan didn't suppress the curse this time. He let it rip. He knew what had happened. He had told her she couldn't go to that gambling den she had mentioned, and she didn't like it when anyone said "No" to her. So she had pretended to go along with him, then slipped out of the room as soon as she got the chance.

She hadn't even waited until it was more likely that he was asleep. That was how sure of herself she was.

Angrily, Logan went back to his room and pulled the rest of his clothes back on. He strapped the Colt's cross-draw rig to his belt and settled his hat on his head. Then he took his cane and headed downstairs.

The clerk at the desk in the lobby looked surprised when Logan asked if he had seen Gillian. "Miss Baldwin?" the man said. He shook his head. "Not at all, sir. I was under the impression she was in her father's regular suite."

"That's where she should be," Logan said. "Can you get buggies in front of the hotel?"

"Of course, although there are fewer at this time of night."

Logan nodded curt thanks and turned toward the hotel's front door.

"Do you need some help, sir?" the clerk called after him.

"Probably," Logan muttered under his breath, but he didn't pause or turn around.

He went outside and leaned on his cane as he waited for a buggy for hire to come along. Several minutes later, a vehicle drawn by a tired-looking horse came along the street and drew up in front of the hotel when Logan waved his cane at the driver.

"You need to go somewhere, mister?" the driver asked in deep, slow tones.

"Do you know a gambling house called Michael's?" Logan asked. "It's supposed to be a pretty fancy place."

"Michael's," the driver repeated. "Can't say as I – Wait a minute. You ain't talkin' about Red Mike's, are you?"

"I don't know. It's supposed to be a place where there's gambling and drinking and dancing, and it's in an old mansion somewhere in town."

"That'd be Red Mike's," the man said. "I ain't sure it'd be a good idea for you to be goin' there, sir. It can get kinda rough, and with you bein' . . . well . . ."

"I know I'm crippled," Logan snapped. He brought his anger under control and went on, "I'm sorry. But this Red Mike's would be a bad place for a young woman to go alone, wouldn't it? A well brought up young woman?"

"Yes, mister, it sure would," the driver said.

Logan reached for the buggy seat. "Take me there," he said.

"You sure about that?"

"I don't have any choice in the matter."

* * *

Logan's anger had subsided somewhat and he was cooler-headed by the time the cab reached the big, old plantation house on the outskirts of Little Rock. The driver explained, "Used to be a fine family owned this place before the war. Some of my kinfolks worked here. Slaves, you know. But they was plenty who had it worse. Then the war come along and wiped 'em out. Carpetbagger fella, Irishman name of Michael Carnahan, came in and took it over, turned it into a place for rich folks to drink and gamble and do whatever unsavory things they took it into their minds to do. Got to be rougher and rougher and some of the rich folks stopped comin'. Now it's mostly just trash, but sometimes somebody from the better classes wanders in. They got that curiosity, you know, 'bout how all them squalid lower class folks live. I've heard some stories . . ."

The driver's voice trailed off, and he shook his head.

"What's your name?" Logan asked.

"They call me Deacon, sir, on account of I been known to preach the word of the Lord when the spirit's on me."

"I appreciate you helping me, Deacon. I'll see to it that you're well paid if you'll wait for me outside the place."

"I can do that," Deacon said. "I can go in with you if you want. Some of the folks in there won't like it, but I'll do it if you need me to."

"The former Confederates, you mean?"

Deacon snorted and said, "Them, too, but mostly them northern carpetbaggers. Didn't take me long after they got here for me to figure out they done hate us worse'n southern folks do. War wasn't much more'n an excuse for them to come in and take over ever'thing from the plantations to the big businesses. Reckon it's good that we ain't slaves no more, but if'n you look around, you'll see that most of us ain't all that much better off. Anyway, you see how come I took to preachin'." He laughed. "I'm just naturally long-winded, I reckon."

"Well, you just wait out here," Logan said as he climbed out of the buggy. "We may have to leave in a hurry. I hope it doesn't come to that, but if it does . . ."

"I'll be ready," Deacon said.

A number of wagons, buggies, carriages, and saddle horses were tied up in front of the plantation house. A few drivers lounged with their vehicles, smoking quirlies. Logan limped past them and went toward the front door, which had a cornice lamp burning on either side of it. The door was open, and he heard music and laughter coming from beyond it.

A stocky man in an ill-fitting suit waited just inside the door. "Cost you six bits to come in," he said.

Logan handed the man a silver dollar and said, "I'm looking for a woman – "

"Plenty of 'em here, but you'll have to make your own arrangements with them," the man said. "We don't do that. Liable to cost you extra, you bein' a gimp and all."

Logan reined in his temper. The man had an Irish accent, so he asked, "Are you Red Mike?"

"Me? Carnahan?" The man laughed. "Hell, no. I just work for the lad. You'll know him when you see him. Hair like flame, he's got."

Logan moved past the man at the door. Beyond the foyer was a short entrance hall that had been turned into a bar. Past it were double doors opening into a ballroom that was now a gambling den. As Logan moved into the room, he saw roulette wheels, faro layouts, poker and blackjack tables. The place was crowded, and the players were the mixture he expected: a few well-dressed men and women, out for the excitement of doing something dangerous, and the others dressed in rougher clothing with the lines of harder, more desperate lives etched on their faces.

Logan didn't see Gillian Baldwin anywhere.

But in a crowd like this, it was difficult to take in everything at once. He began making his way around the room, his eyes narrow under the brim of his hat as he searched for her.

He heard her before he saw her. The familiar voice held a note of panic as she said, "No, please, I don't want to – "

"We had a bet, remember?" a man said. "It's not my fault you told the dealer to hit you again on seventeen. Now you got to pay up."

"You took my money – " Gillian said.

"Money wasn't all you were betting, and you knew it."

With his pulse beginning to hammer in his head, Logan moved around a clump of people blocking his view and saw Gillian being forced up a curving staircase at the side of the room. The man who had hold of her arm was dressed in a white suit, had dark hair that was slightly askew and a mustache. From the way the man's face was flushed, Logan thought he might be drunk . . .

155

but not too drunk to know what he was doing.

Gillian had changed into a much more provocative gown before sneaking out of the hotel. It wasn't cut quite as low as the one she had worn to the party the night before, but almost. She was beautiful, but she was also scared. She had tried to do something daring but had wound up in trouble instead.

For a second, Logan was tempted to turn around, walk out of Red Mike's, and leave her to whatever was going to happen. She had brought this on herself, after all, with her vain, arrogant stubbornness.

But he knew he couldn't do that, so he moved as quickly as he could to the foot of the stairs and called, "Gillian!"

The room was so noisy that she might not be able to hear him. But her head snapped around toward him and he knew she had. So had the man who was trying to make her go upstairs with him. He paused, turned his head to scowl down at Logan, and demanded, "Who the hell are you?"

"I'm that lady's friend," Logan said, "and I want you to let go of her."

"Yeah, well, you can go to hell," the man rasped. "She lost a bet to me, and now she's got to pay up."

"I . . . I never bet what you're saying I did," Gillian said. "This is all a misunderstanding – "

"I don't think so. Come on."

The man tugged on her arm again. Gillian struggled but couldn't pull free. Logan started up the stairs toward the two of them. He couldn't move very fast.

The man saw him coming and shoved Gillian down beside him. He turned with an angry grimace contorting his face.

"I don't like to fight cripples," he said, "but this won't be much of a fight."

He lunged down the stairs at Logan.

20.

The drunken, amorous gambler was right about one thing: it wasn't much of a fight.

Logan tipped the cane up and rammed it into the man's stomach. The man's own momentum worked against him, making the blow even more effective as the cane jabbed into his belly. He started to double over, his eyes widening in unexpected pain. Since the man was already off-balance, Logan lowered the cane, thrust it between his ankles, and twisted. With a wild yell, the man toppled forward. Logan pivoted out of the way so that the man somersaulted past him and down the rest of the staircase, out of control, until he wound up in a stunned heap at the base of the stairs.

The altercation drew the attention of quite a few people in the big room. Logan didn't like that; he would have preferred to get Gillian out of here quietly, without making a scene. Keeping her safe was his main job, but he figured Marcus Baldwin might not be too pleased if Little Rock started buzzing with gosspip about his daughter.

He moved up four steps to where she sat on one of the risers, looking shaken. "Are you all right?" he asked.

"Yes, I . . ." She had to stop for a second before she could go on. "I didn't expect to run into such trouble here."

"You might have if you'd taken the time to find out what sort of reputation this place really has," he said. He didn't bother trying to keep the irritation out of his voice.

She looked up at him and said, "I'm so glad you found me, Logan. I don't know what would have happened if you hadn't shown up when you did."

"I don't think either of us wants to know."

A couple of burly men in poorly fitting suits like the man at the door approached the fallen gambler. Another man trailed behind them. He was better dressed, and his red hair told Logan that he was probably Michael Carnahan . . . or Red Mike, as he was known in some quarters.

"Get him out of here," the redhaired man told his subordinates. "Don't damage him too much, but make sure he remembers in the future that it's not wise to cause trouble in my place." He came up a couple of steps toward Logan and Gillian as the bruisers dragged the white-suited man away. "Is the lady all right?"

"I'm fine," Gillian said stiffly. Logan figured she was trying to regain some of her lost dignity. She lifted a hand to him and went on, "Help me up, Mr. Handley."

Logan did so, and when Gillian was on her feet again, she descended the stairs regally. The hum of normal conversation began again in the room. The show, such as it had been, was over.

When the three of them were at the bottom of the staircase, Carnahan said, "I'd like to buy both of you a drink, Miss . . . ?"

Logan didn't give her a chance to answer. He wanted to keep the Baldwin name out of this affair. He said, "We're obliged to you, but that won't be necessary. We're leaving."

"Already?" Carnahan murmured. "I was hoping this

unfortunate unpleasantness could be forgotten – "

Logan shook his head and said, "We hold no grudges, but I think it would be best if we left."

"Logan, please," Gillian said. "We're already here, and I'm sure there won't be any more trouble."

"I give you my word on that," Carnahan said.

Logan hesitated. Arguing with Gillian might draw more unwanted attention. After a moment he shrugged and said, "I suppose it wouldn't hurt anything to stay a while longer. But only a little while."

"Excellent." Carnahan linked arms with Gillian, then glanced at Logan. "With your permission, sir . . ."

"You don't need my permission," Logan said. "Only the lady's."

"Thank you," Gillian told Carnahan with one of her dazzling smiles. "I've already tried blackjack. What other games do you recommend?"

"What about roulette? It can be very exciting."

"Yes, I'd love to try that," Gillian said.

Logan followed them as they headed for one of the roulette tables. He had spent a lot of time in smoky gambling dens such as this one, so the place held no novelty for him. He supposed it was new and exciting to Gillian, though.

Almost too exciting, he thought wryly.

In the next half-hour, as Gillian won and lost at the roulette wheel and seemed to be having a good time with Carnahan at her side and Logan waiting nearby, a couple of fights broke out in other parts of the room. They attracted only momentary interest before Red Mike's bouncers moved in quickly to break them up. Evidently violence was nothing unusual here, which came as no surprise to Logan since he had heard about the place's reputation from Deacon.

He hoped the black man was still waiting outside with the buggy. Finding another here on the outskirts of town might prove to be difficult at this time of night.

Logan couldn't have said what it was that made him stiffen suddenly as the skin on the back of his neck crawled. He knew his instincts were warning him about *something*, but as he looked around the room, he didn't see anything threatening.

Then a couple of people moved, creating a grap in the crowd, and he got a good view of a poker table he hadn't been able to see a moment earlier. The table was about thirty feet away from him. One of the players seated on the other side of the table, facing him, was a man with a black hat tipped far back on his thick black hair. The man's face was instantly familiar to Logan.

Jim Meadows.

But there was something different, and for a second Logan wasn't sure if the man was Meadows after all. He realized that this man had an ugly scar on the right side of his face, leading back toward his ear. Meadows hadn't had a scar like that the last time Logan had seen him . . .

Christmas Eve. The office of the Rimfire Mining Syndicate in Aspen Creek, Montana. A shot from a derringer that made blood fly from Meadows' head . . .

The mining syndicate office had been empty when men got there after Logan stopped the dynamite from blowing up the town hall, but there was quite a bit of blood on the floor. Logan had had problems of his own to occupy his mind, but when he thought about Meadows' disappearance, he hoped that the gunman had crawled off somewhere and died.

Clearly, that hadn't been the case, because Jim Meadows was alive and well, if scarred, in Red Mike's gambling den here in Little Rock, Arkansas. Logan had no doubt that's who he was looking at.

Had Meadows followed him to Arkansas? That seemed unlikely, but Logan couldn't rule it out. Meadows had always been a vain man. He would want revenge for the wound that had ruined his looks. The way Logan had interfered with his plans in Montana would be just one more score to settle.

But it was certainly possible that Meadows' presence was just a coincidence. Wilder things had happened.

Meadows' attention was focused on the cards in his hand. He hadn't looked up from them in the handful of seconds it took for those thoughts to go through Logan's mind. Without hurrying or doing anything to draw interest, Logan turned so that Meadows wouldn't be able to see his face. He angled toward the spot where Gillian was standing with Mike Carnahan, still playing roulette.

The wheel made a whirring sound as it spun around. The little white ball clattered and clicked. It finally fell and came to a stop in one of the slots. Logan didn't even look to see which one it was. He could tell by Gillian's reaction that she was excited and happy.

"You're going to have to quit while you're ahead," he told her. "We need to leave."

"Leave?" she repeated. "But I'm just getting started!"

"You've had a taste of the experience. That'll have to be enough."

Her mouth hardened into an angry line as she said, "I don't recall my father telling you that you can give me orders."

"Your father told me to keep you safe, and I can do a better job of that if you're back at the hotel in his suite."

Carnahan said, "I think the lady's old enough to make up her own mind, mister."

Logan gave the redheaded man a cold stare. "She's already run into trouble here once tonight. I don't want it happening again."

"Nobody's bothering me," Gillian snapped. "Everything is perfectly fine."

Except that it wasn't. Jim Meadows was here. And in all likelihood, Meadows could still pull a gun with the same speed he always had. The bullet crease that had left his face scarred didn't look like it would have affected his vision. He would be as fast and deadly as ever.

And Logan wasn't. A showdown with Meadows tonight would be a death sentence.

He didn't want to beg, but he was already a coward for wanting to run, so what did it matter, he asked himself. He said quietly, "Please, we need to go now. It's important."

Gillian pouted for a moment, but then she shrugged and said, "Oh, all right, if it means that much to you." She turned to Carnahan and went on, "How much money do I have coming as my winnings, Michael?"

"A little over three hundred dollars," Carnahan said.

Practically the same amount of money Baldwin had offered him for this job, Logan thought. Carnahan didn't look that happy at the thought of paying it out, either.

"Why don't I leave it here with you?" Gillian said. "Then I'll have some money to play with starting out, the next time I'm here."

That idea pleased Carnahan more. There was always a chance Gillian would never be back, or would forget about the money, and then he'd never have to pay it out.

"All right," he said, "but I hope that's not long."

"I'm sure it won't be."

Logan moved up next to her, keeping his back turned

toward the table where he had spotted Jim Meadows, and touched her arm with his left hand.

"Let's go," he said.

She smiled and came with him, but as they started making their way toward the entrance, she asked under her breath, "What's got you so worked up, Logan?"

"I just think we've pushed our luck as far as we ought to tonight," he told her. "That's what my instincts say, anyway, and I've learned to trust them."

He burned inside with shame at the thought of fleeing from an old enemy like this, and lying to Gillian about it just made things worse. But in a way he was doing the right thing, he told himself. If Meadows killed him, then Gillian would be left here alone, and he was confident that wouldn't turn out well.

He got his hat and the coat Gillian had worn and led her outside. Thankfully, Deacon and the buggy were waiting in the same place where he had left them.

"Back to the hotel," Logan told the driver as he helped Gillian into the rear seat.

"Yes, sir," Deacon said, and Logan thought he sounded quite relieved.

But no more relieved than he was. Tonight had been a close call in more ways than one. Logan knew he couldn't count on his luck continuing. Sooner or later he would have to face his past.

But not tonight. Thankfully, not tonight.

21.

Logan sat back in the big stone tub and let the hot water flow around him. It smelled a little of sulfur, which he thought was appropriate. Brimstone for a killer.

Tiny swirls of steam curled from the water's surface. The heat felt good as it soaked into Logan's muscles. It was especially welcome now that winter had settled in and the weather was dank and chilly most of the time. There was no doubt in Logan's mind that the mineral bath treatments he had been taking for the past few weeks were pleasant. Very pleasant, in fact.

But he couldn't tell that they they had done a blasted thing to strengthen his arm and leg.

The lack of progress was frustrating. Dr. Strittmatter claimed that it was simply a matter of time, that Logan hadn't given the treatments long enough to work yet. Maybe he was right; Logan was no doctor, so it was hard for him to be sure about such things.

But the suspicious side of his mind asked him what else Strittmatter was going to say. The doctor charged him for every one of these treatments, so naturally it was to Strittmatter's advantage to keep Logan and all his other patients returning time after time.

After a while, a large, bald man named Gunther came into the room and announced, "Time for your massage now, *Herr* Handley."

Gunther had come to America with Dr. Strittmatter, Logan supposed. On every visit, after soaking in the bath, Logan climbed onto a hard table and lay there face down while Gunther massaged his arm and leg. Again, it felt good, but Logan wasn't sure it was actually helping.

Today as he lay there on the table while Gunther worked on him, his thoughts drifted back over the past few weeks. Since returning from Little Rock with Gillian, Logan had done a few more small jobs for Marcus Baldwin, all of which involved guarding sums of money. Some of it had gone to Little Rock, and some had been delivered to logging camps in the Ouachita Mountains. Logan hadn't encountered any problems during the trips. His life, in fact, had become rather boring. Gillian seemed to be staying close to home these days. Maybe the train holdup and the close shave at the gambling den had spooked her more than she let on.

The good thing was that Baldwin had continued to be generous with his wages, so Logan was able to afford the treatments at Dr. Strittmatter's bathhouse and also had been able to move out of Vickie Eastland's boarding house and take a room at one of the less expensive hotels. Eventually he planned to rent a house of his own.

It was a relief knowing that any dangers from his past wouldn't be menacing Vickie, Rusty, or anyone else who lived at the boarding house. He couldn't deny that he missed all of them, however. Especially Vickie . . .

Whenever that thought crossed his mind, he told himself he was being foolish. Really, Vickie had never been anything more than civil to him. He had been just another boarder to her, that was all.

When Gunther was finished with the massage, Logan wrapped himself in a thick robe and went back to the room where he had hung up his clothes and his gun. He got dressed, took his cane, and limped out of the bathhouse.

For some reason, his steps turned toward the barber shop. He hadn't seen Doc Reese for a while, so he decided to stop there and say hello. He might even go across the street to Dumont's and get a drink while he was in that part of town, he told himself.

Oddly enough, stepping into the barber shop felt a little like coming home. He wasn't sure why he felt that way, since he hadn't really worked there for very long. But there was a grin on his face anyway as he went past the striped pole and entered the building.

Doc didn't have any customers at the moment. He was sitting in the chair himself with a newspaper spread open in front of him. He glanced up, looked over the paper, and said, "If you've come for a haircut, I think I can squeeze you in if you don't mind waiting."

Logan chuckled. "Actually, I just came by to say hello, but I suppose I could use a trim."

Doc folded the paper, set it aside, and got out of the chair. He picked up the cape folded over the arm of the chair and motioned for Logan to sit down. Logan did so after hanging up his hat.

"I won't even ask you to sweep up afterward," Doc said as he fastened the cape around Logan's neck. "How are you doing?"

"All right, I suppose."

"Still working for Marcus Baldwin?"

"Part of the time. Whenever he has something for me to do."

Doc grunted over the *snick-snick* of the scissors as he got to work. He said, "I noticed you weren't limping as bad when you came in just now."

"I've been going to Dr. Strittmatter's bathhouse for treatments," Logan said. "I thought they weren't really helping, but maybe they are and I just can't see the progress because I'm too close to it."

Doc snorted. "There's nothing wrong with a hot mineral bath," he said. "It'll make you feel better for a while. But the thing that's made your leg stronger and helped your limp is walking up and down these hills. All that exercise can't help but strengthen your muscles. I told you that the first time we met."

"I don't know, Doc . . ."

"Think about it," Doc said. "Your arm isn't any better, is it?"

"Not that I can tell," Logan admitted.

"That's because you never did those exercises I recommended to you. You're not using it enough. You got in the habit of favoring it after you were afflicted, and you've never gotten over that. You've got to make an effort to exercise it more."

Maybe Doc had a point, Logan mused. He thought back over the past few weeks. He hadn't thought that his leg was getting better because there hadn't been any dramatic changes in it. Yet Doc had noticed an improvement in his limp right away. Doc hadn't seen him in a while, so he could tell a difference. And now that Logan thought about it, he didn't think he was quite as tired and his leg didn't ache as badly whenever he got back to the hotel from walking around town.

If Doc was right, then paying Strittmatter to sit in a tub of hot, stinking water was sort of like throwing money away, other than the relaxation Logan got out of it. He wasn't sure that was worth what the doctor was charging him.

"What do you think I should do to help my arm, Doc?"

"Well . . ." Doc paused and grinned. "It might do some

good if you were to grab that broom in the corner and sweep for a while."

Logan laughed. "I thought you weren't going to make me do that."

"Just giving you some friendly advice, that's all."

Doc finished with the haircut, untied the cape, powdered and brushed off the back of Logan's neck. While Doc was doing that, the shop door opened again, and Rusty Turner came in.

"I was hopin' I might find you here, Logan," he said. "I been by the hotel where you're stayin' now, and that little foreign fella's bathhouse. Howdy, Doc."

"Hello, Rusty," Doc said. "You seem a bit distracted."

"I'm all right. Logan, Mr. Baldwin sent me to find you."

"He's got something else for me to do?" Logan asked.

"I dunno. He don't confide in me. But he seemed upset about somethin'."

"Looks like I won't have a chance to sweep up after all, Doc," Logan said as he stood up.

"That's all right," Doc said. "Just remember what I told you about that arm. Start using it more, and you'll see a change in it. Just be prepared for it being sore, like I warned you about from the start."

Logan nodded, settled his hat on his head, and left the shop with Rusty.

As they walked through the blustery day toward Baldwin's office, Logan said, "Rusty, do you think I'm limping as bad as I used to?"

Rusty frowned in thought as he turned his head to watch Logan's gait for a moment before he replied. "Maybe not quite as much," he said.

"Doc noticed it right away because he hadn't seen me in a while. He says my leg is finally getting stronger because of all the walking I do up and down the hills here in Hot Springs."

"It's a hilly place, I'll give it that," Rusty agreed. "He still don't believe the mineral baths will cure what ails you?"

"He says they won't do anything except make the muscles feel better temporarily."

"Well, if you're hurtin' bad enough, that'd be worth somethin' by itself."

"I suppose so," Logan agreed. "I won't deny that the baths feel good. But Doc claims only exercise will make my muscles stronger."

Rusty shook his head and said, "When it comes to doctorin', I don't know a blessed thing. But I know Doc Reese is a smart man. I'd be tempted to follow his advice, if I was you."

Logan nodded. "That's exactly what I'm thinking about doing. But right now I guess I need to find out what Mr. Baldwin wants before I do anything else."

Upon their arrival, they were shown immediately into Marcus Baldwin's office. This time Rusty was allowed in, too. He said, "I brung him just like you said to, Mr. Baldwin."

"Yes, thank you, Turner," Baldwin said, clearly distracted by something. He waved Logan into the well-padded chair in front of the desk. Rusty fidgeted for a couple of seconds, then said goodbye to Logan and left the office. If he had hoped for a more concrete expression of Baldwin's gratitude, he would just have to be disappointed.

"I've gotten some disturbing reports from my logging camps in the past couple of days, Logan," Baldwin went on. "There's been some sabotage – supplies destroyed, mysterious fires, my men shot at – and I want you to look into it. You've handled jobs like that in the past, haven't you?"

"Yes, sir, I have," Logan admitted, "but that was when I was able-bodied and could stay in the saddle all day when I was following a trail, if I needed to."

"The roads are good enough that a buggy can manage on most of them. You can handle a buggy, can't you?"

"Not and do any shooting at the same time, if it comes to that," Logan replied bluntly. An idea came to him. "But I might be able to look into the situation if you send Rusty with me to drive."

"Turner?" Baldwin frowned. "I suppose I could do that. He's a good man, but certainly not indispensible to my freight operation down here. I'll call him back in here."

"First, why don't you tell me exactly what's happened?"

"I'll do better than that. I'll let you read the reports for yourself."

Baldwin pushed several sheets of paper across the desk. Logan picked them up and started to read. He saw that the problems were just as Baldwin had described them.

"Seems like most of the trouble is centered around the Devil's Gorge camp," he said. "That's where I'd start looking."

"Handle things however you see fit," Baldwin said. "Just put a stop to Nash's mischief."

"You think Aaron Nash is behind this?"

Baldwin snorted in disgust and said, "Who else could it be? No one else has any reason to want to cause trouble for me. Nash thinks his hired guns will undermine my operation until I quit and leave all the timber for him. He should know better. That's never going to happen."

Baldwin's mention of hired guns made Logan think of Jim Meadows. He hadn't seen Meadows since that night in Little Rock. Obviously the scar-faced gunman wasn't trying to track him down after all, or else Meadows would have shown up in Hot Springs by now.

But it was possible that Meadows might be working for Aaron Nash without even knowing that Logan was anywhere in the area. The sort of sabotage described in the reports was just the sort of thing Meadows would be involved in. At its heart, this conflict between Baldwin and Nash was no different than all the range wars in which Meadows had been hired by one side or the other . . . and Logan, too.

Logan knew it would take several hours to reach the Devil's Gorge camp, but it was still early enough in the day to make it by nightfall. He got to his feet and said, "I'll go find Rusty. We'll leave as soon as possible."

"Good." Baldwin still seemed worried and distracted, and Logan wondered suddenly if the man's financial situation was more precarious than he let on. Baldwin certainly appeared to have plenty of money, but Logan had seen in the past that such businessmen usually put up that façade even when they were having trouble. *Especially* when they were having trouble, he thought, because they didn't want any of their enemies sensing a potential weakness.

Logan started to leave the office, but then he paused and asked, "How's Miss Baldwin?"

"Gillian? She's fine. I don't really see much of her these days. She has a new beau, and as usual, she's all caught up in that."

"First I've heard of it," Logan said, then immediately felt a little foolish. There was no reason for him to keep up with Gillian Baldwin's social life.

"It won't last," Baldwin said with a dismissive wave. "None of Gillian's little flirtations do."

Her flirtation with *him* hadn't lasted, Logan thought, but that was because he had never allowed it to get out of hand. Even if he had, he was sure Gillian would have tired of him in a hurry.

The novelty of romancing a cripple had to be pretty short-lived.

Without saying anything else, he left the office and went next door to the barn to look for Rusty. He would need to go back to the hotel and get his shotgun, too, and it might be a good idea for Rusty to bring along a rifle or a handgun. Or both.

If they found the men who were causing the trouble, they were liable to wind up needing all the firepower they could muster.

22.

The city of Hot Springs and the area around it were a federal reservation, having been made so years earlier by a declaration from President Andrew Jackson, a believer in the healing properties of the water from the springs. But the heavily forested Ouachita Mountains, west and northwest of the town, were not federal property, and in recent years the thick growth of loblolly pines had attracted the burgeoning timber industry, represented primarily by Marcus Baldwin and Aaron Nash.

Devil's Gorge Camp was located some twenty miles northwest of Hot Springs and took its name from a deep, steep-sided, brush-choked ravine that ran nearby. Baldwin kept a full crew of loggers there, and they stayed busy trimming and felling pines that were then cut up into manageable sections, loaded onto big wagons pulled by mule teams made up of a dozen or more of the beasts, and hauled to Little Rock to be milled into lumber and paper. Baldwin's long-range plans called for building a mill closer to the mountains and the timber supply, but that was still in the future.

Logan already knew some of this and learned the rest from listening to the talkative Rusty Turner during the drive to Devil's Gorge Camp. As they neared there late that afternoon, Rusty was still talking. Logan suddenly leaned forward in the buggy seat, held up a hand to stop him, and said, "Hold on a minute. Stop the buggy."

Rusty hauled back on the reins. As the buggy halted, the rattle of its wheels died away. The thick forest that pressed in on both sides of the trail swallowed up any echoes. Silence hung over the mountains.

"That ain't right," Rusty said. "There should be some noise from the animals – "

A sudden burst of gunfire shattered the quiet. That explained why the inhabitants of the forest had all fallen silent. Logan had thought a moment earlier that he heard shots. That was why he had spoken up. At first when everything was still after Rusty stopped the buggy, he had wondered if he was mistaken.

Now he knew there had just been a lull in the shooting. Now it had started up again, the reports coming furiously.

Rusty let out a startled curse. "Sounds like somebody's goin' to war!" he said.

"You've been up here before," Logan said. "Are those shots coming from the direction of Baldwin's camp?"

"They sure as blazes are!"

"Get us there as fast as you can," Logan ordered, his voice grim. He reached down to the floorboard where the wooden case containing the scattergun was resting between his feet and picked it up.

Rusty slapped the reins against the backs of the two horses pulling the buggy and called out to them. The horses broke into a trot. The faster pace meant the vehicle bounced and rocked more, but that didn't matter. Logan wanted to reach the logging camp as quickly as possible. He hung on to one of the struts that supported the buggy's canvas top.

Rusty wheeled the buggy around a bend in the trail. Several buildings came into view. Logan had been up here before and recognized the long bunkhouse, the mess hall, and its attached cook shack. Across the big clearing where the camp was located loomed the large, open-sided, covered shed where logs were stored until they could be hauled off to the mills. Next to it was the tool shed where the axes, saws, climbing gear, and other equipment were kept.

Spurts of powdersmoke came from the sheds. Answering shots roared from the windows of the bunkhouse as Rusty reined in. If he'd kept going, he and Logan would have wound up directly between the two forces, in the middle of that furious, lethal crossfire.

The buggy skidded to a halt. Logan and Rusty piled out of the vehicle. Logan had the scattergun in his right hand by now. Rusty grabbed the Henry rifle he had brought with him. They took cover behind the buggy as a bullet whined over their heads.

"How can we tell which side is ours?" Rusty asked. "We can't see any of 'em. They're all behind cover!"

"Did you see which direction that shot came from? I think we can assume that anybody trying to ventilate us isn't our friend!"

"No, dadgum it, I didn't. With everybody blazin' away, it's hard to tell."

Rusty was right about that. Logan hadn't been able to tell which side had fired the shot, either. That left him with no choice but to try to draw another one.

"Watch the shed," he told Rusty. "I'll keep an eye on the bunkhouse."

"What're you gonna – Damn it, Logan, be careful!"

Too late for that, Logan thought as he stepped out into the open where the men in the shed and those in the bunkhouse could see him.

Almost instantly, another jet of gunsmoke came from one of the bunkhouse windows. Logan felt the wind-rip of the bullet as it passed close to his ear. He dived back behind the buggy.

"You nearly got your dang fool head blowed off!" Rusty exclaimed.

"Yeah, but now we know it's probably not Mr. Baldwin's men holed up in the bunkhouse."

"You can't be sure about that. They maybe mistook us for some more of whoever they're shootin' at."

Unfortunately, Rusty was right, Logan realized. Still, the odds favored the men in the shed being Baldwin's loggers. This was just about the right time for them to return to the camp after putting in a day's work. Maybe they had found somebody skulking around the bunkhouse. Logan recalled reading in some of the reports that there had been some mysterious fires.

Anybody who would start a fire in a forest like this was risking incredible destruction. The blaze could spread and engulf many square miles of trees. The fact that none of the fires had done much damage so far was a combination of quick action by the loggers in putting them out and sheer luck.

But someone taking the long view might be willing to risk it. Nature would repair the devastation. The trees would grow back. Aaron Nash might be willing to pay such a price to put Marcus Baldwin out of business.

Those thoughts flashed through Logan's mind. He knew it was all sheer speculation at this point, and he didn't really have the time to spend on it. He pointed and said to Rusty, "If we can get into the woods over there, we can circle through them and make it to the sheds."

"I can make a run for it," Rusty said, "but you can't, Logan. The way the buggy's parked, it'd shield you a little from the bunkhouse, but you'd still be out in the open too long. They'd be liable to drill you."

"It's a chance I've got to take," Logan said.

Rusty couldn't talk him out of it. The older man said, "If you're gonna do it, at least let me cover you. I'll spray the front of that bunkhouse with so much lead, nobody'll have a chance to draw a bead on you."

Logan thought about it and nodded. "All right, and I'll cover you from the trees once I've made it over there."

"That's long range for a handgun."

"I don't care if I hit anything. I just want to make them keep their heads down."

Rusty grinned and said, "That sounds like a pretty good plan, if you're bound and determined to do it."

"I am. Let's go."

Rusty worked the Henry's lever. "Whenever you're ready."

Logan had grabbed the cane with his left hand when he got out of the buggy, but he was going to need it in his right hand while he tried to hurry into the trees. He switched hands with the cane and the shotgun. The weapon was heavier and put more of a strain on his weakened muscles, but he closed his hand around the stock as tightly as he could and willed himself to hang on.

At that moment he wished he had paid more attention to Doc Reese's advice a long time ago. If he had, maybe his arm would be stronger by now.

But it was too late for that. As Rusty's rifle began to crack, Logan lurched into motion, using the cane for support as he hobbled toward the trees.

Rusty slammed shot after shot at the bunkhouse as fast as he could work the Henry's lever. Logan glanced over his shoulder and saw a couple of puffs of powdersmoke from the windows, but the shots must not have come anywhere close. He didn't hear the bullets as they passed by.

Of course, people said you never heard the bullet that killed you, either, but Logan had never seen how anybody could possibly know that.

The buggy had stopped right where the woods began to widen out into the broad clearing where the camp was located. The closest trees were about fifty feet away. That distance seemed more like fifty miles to Logan as he tried to cover it. He kept moving, expecting to feel the shock of a bullet at any second, but he didn't. He drew closer to the trees, and suddenly he was among them. He lurched behind a thick-trunked pine and rested his back against it for a moment, heedless of any sap he might get on his coat. His heart slugged heavily in his chest, and he couldn't seem to get enough air into his lungs.

Rusty was still over crouched behind the buggy, he reminded himself. Still in danger. Logan dragged in a couple more deep breaths, then leaned the cane against the tree and pulled his Colt from its cross-draw rig. He turned, propped himself up with his left shoulder against the trunk, and called to Rusty, "I made it! I'll cover you!"

Rusty turned to look and raised a hand to wave acknowledgment. At that moment, he jerked and stumbled. He started to fall, and Logan knew his friend had been hit.

Rusty didn't go all the way to the ground. He caught himself on the Henry's butt and used the rifle to lever himself upright again. "I'm all right!" he shouted, then broke into an unsteady run toward the trees.

Logan knew good and well that Rusty wasn't all right. He'd been wounded. But he was moving pretty well again, so Logan leveled the Colt at the bunkhouse, pulled back the hammer, and fired. He saw splinters fly from the sill of the window at which he'd been aiming, so he knew he had come pretty close, especially using a handgun at relatively long range. He'd always been a good shot, and there was nothing wrong with his aim.

He had only six rounds in the Colt – knowing that there might be trouble, he had loaded the sixth chamber, which normally he would have kept empty so the hammer could rest on it – instead of the fifteen that Rusty's Henry held, so he had to be careful and space out his shots more. But by the time Rusty reached the trees without further mishap, Logan had emptied the Colt. He swung around behind the tree trunk again and set the scattergun on the ground so he could reload.

Rusty leaned against another tree and tried to catch his breath. Logan saw blood on his left sleeve and asked, "How bad are you hit?"

"Bullet barely nicked me," Rusty replied. "Hurt like blazes at the time and I reckon the arm will be pretty stiff and sore by tomorrow, but I'll be all right. As soon as I get a chance I'll tie a rag around it to stop the bleedin'."

"Better take the time to do that now," Logan said. "You don't want to pass out from losing too much blood. I've seen it happen."

Rusty took the advice and tore a strip of cloth off the bottom of his shirt to fashion a crude bandage. With the help of his teeth to hold one end, he tied it tightly around the wounded arm. Then he thumbed fresh cartridges into the Henry to replace the ones he had fired.

A few shots from the bunkhouse had torn through the branches around them, but the men holed up in the long, low structure seemed to have forgotten about them for the most part. Logan thought they could risk moving again, especially if they faded back farther into the woods where they wouldn't be seen as easily.

He explained the plan to Rusty, who agreed and said, "Just be careful when we get to the shed. We still don't know exactly what's goin' on here."

"I don't intend to rush into anything," Logan said. He laughed humorlessly and added, "I can't exactly rush, anyway."

They circled through the trees. It would be easy to get lost in such thick growth. Here under the spreading branches was perpetual gloom, since not much sunlight ever penetrated this far. Fallen needles carpeted the ground. There wasn't a great deal of undergrowth to impede their progress.

The sound of gunfire guided them, and after a few minutes they reached a spot behind the shed, across the clearing from the bunkhouse. From where they crouched at the edge of the trees, they could see the men who used the piles of logs for cover and fired toward the bunkhouse.

Rusty said, "I recognize two or three of those fellas! They're part of the loggin' crew, all right. We picked the right side, Logan."

"Now we can give them a hand," Logan said. "We'll just have to be careful and not spook them too much when we come up behind them, or they're liable to turn around and – "

He stopped short when some instinct made him look to his left. At first he didn't see anything except tree trunks and branches laden with needles.

But then he realized something was sticking out from behind one of those tree trunks, something long and menacing.

It was a rifle barrel, and whoever was wielding the weapon appeared to be drawing a bead on the loggers in the shed.

23.

Logan had holstered the Colt and had the scattergun in his right hand again. He brought the double-barreled weapon up and triggered the right-hand barrel, sending a load of deadly buckshot slashing through the trees.

"To the left, Rusty!" he warned. Movement among the trunks told him more than one bushwhacker lurked over there.

Rusty's wounded arm didn't hinder him much as he got the Henry cracking again. The rifle fire forced one man into the open, and Logan was waiting for him. The second charge of buckshot caught the would-be bushwhacker and lifted him off his feet, slamming him to the ground in a bloody heap.

Logan dropped the scattergun and pulled the Colt. Return fire thudded into the tree trunk beside him as he crouched. He wasn't even really aware of his bad leg anymore; the blood pounded so hard through his veins that all he cared about was the battle.

God, he had missed it!

The roar of guns, the acrid bite of powdersmoke in his nose, the kick of a revolver against his hand, the knowledge that his life and the lives of other men hung in the balance . . . All those things had been like food and drink to him for so many years. It had been a grim, lonely, desperate life . . . but it had been *his* life.

And now for a moment it was his again.

Until a bullet kicked up dirt right beside him and he

tried to move quickly from one bit of cover to another. When he did, his bad leg went out from under him with no warning and dumped him on the ground between two trees, an easy target.

More dirt spurted from a narrow miss and sprayed in his face, blinding him. He had held on to the Colt and fired by instinct. He hoped that would rattle his enemies if nothing else.

Then a hand grasped his ankle and hauled back. Logan slid over the ground. Rusty pulled him behind a tree and dropped beside him.

"That was too blasted close," Rusty said. "You gotta be more careful, Logan."

"I . . . I forgot for a second . . . forgot I'm not the man I once was – "

"Don't worry about that. I think we got those varmints on the run."

Logan listened. The shooting had diminished. He heard men crashing through what brush there was in the forest. It sounded like they were lighting a shuck out of here.

But not all of the gunmen were ready to give up just yet. Another flurry of shots ripped through the trees. Still flat on his belly, Logan slid to the side and aimed at a muzzle flash in the gloom. Just before he squeezed the trigger, the man fired again, and this time in the glare of orange flame, Logan caught a glimpse of his face.

A split-second later Logan's Colt roared and bucked in his hand, and the man he had aimed at disappeared. Logan didn't know if he'd hit the target or if the gunman had just abandoned the fight after all.

But he was certain he had recognized that scarred face.

Jim Meadows.

Ever since he had spotted Meadows at Red Mike Carnahan's place in Little Rock, Logan had known that he would see the man again. He had always been too hard-headed, too pragmatic, to believe much in fate or destiny or whatever anybody wanted to call it. But despite that, he knew. With him working for one side in this timber war, it was inevitable that Meadows would turn up on the other side.

It was just too damned fitting not to happen.

A few more scattered shots rang out, then silence settled down over the forest again. Rusty opened his mouth to say something, but Logan lifted a hand and motioned for him to stay quiet. They waited.

Several minutes went by, and then a man called, "Hey! In the trees behind the shed! Anybody out there?"

"I know that voice," Rusty whispered. "That's Judd Farley, the foreman of this crew."

Logan nodded. He had met Farley on his previous trip up here to Devil's Gorge Camp. "Go ahead and answer him."

Rusty stood up and shouted, "Hold your fire, Farley! It's Rusty Turner and Logan Handley!"

"Turner!" Farley exclaimed. "What the hell are you doin' out here?"

"Savin' you from gettin' ambushed, from the looks of it," Rusty replied.

After Logan picked up his cane and the scattergun and climbed to his feet, they stepped out of the trees and walked toward the shed. Judd Farley came out to meet them. He was a tall, broad-shouldered man with a shock of prematurely white hair and a bristling mustache. He wore logger's work boots, canvas trousers, and a flannel shirt and carried a single-shot rifle in his big, rough hands.

"What's this about an ambush?" he demanded. "We heard hell break loose back here and figured we were done for, but none of the shots seemed to be comin' in our direction."

"That's because Logan and me kept the devils occupied. We planned to join you in the shed and give you a hand, but Logan spotted ambushers lurkin' in the trees and cut loose on them instead."

Farley nodded to Logan and said, "We're obliged to you, then, Mr. Handley."

"What happened here?" Logan asked.

"We were on our way back in for the day when we heard some shots," Farley said. "Seems that some scoundrels had snuck up and were fixin' to set fire to the bunkhouse. Our cook spotted 'em and went after them with nothin' but a butcher knife and an old cap-and-ball pistol. Old Jonesy never did have a lick of sense. But he managed to chase 'em into the bunkhouse without gettin' himself killed, and he kept 'em pinned down there until we got here. They couldn't set the place on fire while they were in there, so that ruined their plan."

"How'd this bunch get out and get behind you?"

"Varmints chopped a hole in the back wall!" Farley sounded mortally offended by that. "From the looks of it, some of them stayed inside and kept shootin' to make us think they were all in there, while the others snuck around here to catch us in a crossfire. Reckon they hadn't given up on burnin' down the whole camp."

"And we were sneakin' around from the other direction at the same time," Rusty said.

"What happened to the men in the bunkhouse?" Logan asked. He was sure the man he had cut down with the scattergun was dead, but he hoped Farley and the other loggers had gotten their hands on a prisoner or two.

"They all got away," the foreman said disgustedly, dashing that hope.

"That's a shame. I wanted to question one of them. Marcus Baldwin sent us out here to find out who's behind all the trouble you've been having."

"I can tell you that," Farley said with a scowl. "That blasted Aaron Nash, that's who. Nobody else has got it in so bad for Baldwin."

Logan was convinced that Farley was right, but there was still a matter of proof.

With any luck, he could find Jim Meadows and force the man to talk. That would kill the proverbial two birds with one stone.

He could get to the bottom of Baldwin's troubles . . . and he could have his showdown with Meadows at last.

With the hot blood coursing through his veins, Logan didn't even think about the fact that a showdown with Meadows was exactly what he had gone to great pains to avoid a few weeks earlier.

* * *

Aaron Nash was still in his office, working late with his son-in-law Carleton Eastland. Carleton was being particularly obtuse tonight, asking questions about the orders he was being given until Nash finally exploded, "Look, you don't have to *understand* these orders, just pass them along to the men who know what they're doing!"

Eastland frowned and looked offended. "You don't have to take that tone, Aaron – "

"When we're in this office, it's Mr. Nash. You can grasp that, surely."

Eastland nodded stiffly and said, "Of course, Mr. Nash."

A knock sounded on the door that provided a second exit from Nash's private office. It opened into a short hallway that led to an outer door opening in turn into the alley behind the building. Only a few people had keys to that outer door.

Nash drew in a sharp breath. Eastland started toward the door, saying, "Who in the world – "

"That's all!" Nash's harsh words stopped him. Nash went on, "It's late. You can go home, Carleton. Tell Elizabeth I'm sorry I kept you after hours."

Eastland gestured toward the door and said, "But someone – "

"I'll handle it. It's just a routine delivery. I, ah, told them to come around back, since I knew I'd be working late. I left the outer door unlocked."

That was a lie. Nash wasn't expecting anyone. He had a pretty good idea who was on the other side of that door, however, and the so-called routine delivery wouldn't be of good news, that was for sure.

Eastland protested some more, but only half-heartedly. He wanted to go home just as much as his father-in-law wanted him out of there. He said good night and left to get his hat and coat.

Nash went to the rear door and unlocked it.

"Damned well about time," Jim Meadows said when he came in. "I don't like being kept waiting."

"I don't like being interrupted," Nash replied coldly. "What are you doing here?"

"It didn't go like it was supposed to at Devil's Gorge Camp."

"I was afraid that's what you were going to say. What happened?"

"Logan Handley. That's what happened."

Nash frowned and shook his head. "I don't understand."

"Handley and that fella Turner came along and ruined everything. Handley almost put a scar on the other side of my face. I felt the heat of his slug."

"The man's a cripple."

"He sure as hell didn't fight like a cripple. Not today, anyway."

Nash sank down in the chair behind his desk. This competition with Marcus Baldwin was draining him, not just financially but emotionally as well. He was angry and frustrated and wanted to put an end to this.

"When I hired you, you promised to put Baldwin out of business. I told you I didn't care how you went about it, I don't want to know any more of that than I have to, I just want Baldwin dealt with."

"I didn't know I'd be going up against Handley again."

"You can't be afraid of the man!" Nash burst out. "He uses a cane to get around."

"He was moving pretty good today, probably because he wasn't thinking about it."

"His gun arm is no good."

"He can handle a Colt with his off hand. And he's taken to carrying a sawed-off shotgun, too. You don't have to be very slick with a street-sweeper like that."

"If Handley's a problem, deal with him."

"I intend to," Meadows said. He smiled with the unscarred side of his face. "I'm going to give him something else to worry about besides you and Baldwin."

24.

Logan and Rusty searched all around the camp, hoping to find clues that might lead them to some of the other hired gunmen, but they didn't have any luck.

It didn't really matter, Logan told himself. He had the proof of his own eyes that Jim Meadows was involved. Now he had to track down Meadows.

By the time they were approaching Hot Springs in the buggy the next day, Logan's anger had faded some, and his more practical side was trying to assert itself. Meadows was an extremely dangerous man, and while Logan had handled himself better than he expected during the fight the previous day, he wasn't sure if he was ready to take on a killer like Meadows.

But was he ever going to be ready? He couldn't answer that question. Maybe if he kept working at it, he would regain more of the strength in his bad arm and leg, but he would never be back to the way he'd been before the illness felled him. He would have to live with that for the rest of his life and make the best of it.

That life might be considerably shorter if he faced off against Jim Meadows.

He was gazing at the buggy's floorboards and thinking about that when Rusty said, "Hey, look up yonder."

Logan raised his eyes and frowned as he spotted the column of black smoke billowing up into the sky above the valley where Hot Springs was located. They were on the western outskirts of town, and it was obvious that a building was burning somewhere several blocks in front of them.

"Must be quite a blaze," Logan said.

With worry in his voice, Rusty replied, "Looks to me like it's comin' from about where the boardin' house is."

Logan tensed. Rusty was right, he decided as he studied the location of the smoke. Suddenly he was worried, too. Even though he didn't live at the boarding house anymore, he considered all the people who did to be his friends. At this time of day, most of them would be at work . . .

But Vickie wouldn't be. Unless she had gone to the market, Vickie would be at the house.

"Come on," Logan said. "Let's go see."

"Just what I was thinkin'." Rusty snapped the reins and sent the horses trotting ahead briskly. As the buggy drew closer to the smoke he urged them into an outright run.

Logan was sure now that the smoke came from the same block where the Eastland boarding house stood. As they came within sight of the house itself, fear shot through him when he saw black smoke pouring from the windows on the upper stories and flames shooting up from the roof.

Rusty cursed and slashed at the horses' rumps with the reins. Hot Springs had a volunteer fire department, and its wagon was already parked on the street in front of the house with men working the pump handles to send water spraying from a hose handled by a couple of other volunteers. Logan could tell that they weren't going to be able to save the house, though. It was already too far gone.

The street was packed with people watching the fire. As Rusty brought the buggy to a skidding halt before it reached the crowd, Logan looked anxiously among them, hoping to catch a glimpse of Vickie. He didn't see her anywhere.

He spotted several of the boarders he knew and climbed down from the buggy to hurry over to them. "Where's Mrs. Eastland?" he asked. He had to raise his voice to be heard over the crowd commotion and the roaring and crackling of the flames.

The boarders turned to look at him, and one of them, a mostly bald store clerk named Keaton, shook his head and said, "None of us have seen her, Mr. Handley. We were at work and came down here when we heard about the fire."

"We've lost everything in the world," one of the other men said. "Everything."

That was true and Logan knew how terrible they felt, but right now he was more worried about Vickie. He worked his way through the crowd until he could catch hold of the sleeve of the fire department captain.

"Where's Mrs. Eastland?" he asked, again having to shout. "Have you seen Mrs. Eastland?"

"What?" the man snapped distractedly. "Get away, mister! Can't you see we've got our hands full here? We've got to keep that fire from spreading to the other buildings!"

It was true. The firemen had stopped spraying water on the boarding house and were now wetting down the walls and roofs of the neighboring structures. Fire was probably the most feared natural disaster in any frontier town, and Hot Springs was no different.

But was this fire natural? That question suddenly occurred to Logan. He knew how careful Vickie was, how much pride she took in the way she ran her house. The idea of her letting such a blaze start and get so out of hand seemed wrong to him. It wouldn't have happened.

He took a step toward the burning house. He didn't know why. There was nothing he could do. It was an inferno inside; he couldn't go in. But it took an effort of will not to rush into the flames anyway to search for Vickie.

A strong hand closed around his arm. He looked over and saw Rusty standing there.

"It's all right," Logan said. "You don't have to hold me back. I'm not a complete fool."

"I know that," Rusty said, "but you climbed out of the buggy and plunged into the crowd so fast, you forgot this."

He held up Logan's cane.

Logan's eyes widened in surprise. He hadn't realized until this moment that he didn't have the cane, wasn't bracing himself up or helping himself walk with it. He had spent the past few minutes on his own two legs. The right one hurt, but it held him up all right.

Doc Reese was right, he thought. He *was* getting better. His leg was, anyway. And that gave him hope for some eventual improvement in his arm, too.

But right now he didn't really care about that. He said, "I can't find Vickie. Nobody's seen her!"

Before Rusty could respond to that, a familiar voice said, "Logan!"

Relief flooded through him as he turned around sharply and saw her standing there. Several strands of her dark hair had come loose and dangled around her face. Smudges of soot streaked across her forehead and her left cheek. Her eyebrows appeared to have been partially singed off.

Logan thought she was beautiful.

Without thinking about what he was doing, he put his arms around her and drew her against him. She came willingly and pressed her head against his chest. A sob wracked her. She said, "It's gone, all gone!"

"I know," he told her as he held her. "I know. But you're alive and right now that's all that matters."

He comforted her as best he could for several long minutes while the boarding house burned. The roof collapsed, sending more smoke and a towering column of sparks high into the air. Vickie tried to look, but Logan turned so that she couldn't.

"No need for you to see that," he said. "You just hang on to me."

He didn't waste time wondering why she had turned to him in this moment of horrifying loss. It was enough that she had. And because she had, he was determined not to let her down. After a few more moments he slid his good arm around her shoulders and steered her away from the scene of devastation. Rusty followed them, still carrying Logan's cane.

When they reached the edge of the crowd, Rusty lowered the tailgate of a parked wagon and helped Vickie lift herself onto it so she could sit and rest. Logan asked her, "Did everyone get out of the house all right? No one was trapped in there?"

She shook her head. "As far as I know, old Mrs. Parkhurst and I were the only ones in the house when the fire started, and I saw her a few minutes ago. She was worried that *I* hadn't gotten out in time." She lifted a hand and gingerly touched a bloody lump on the side of her head, an injury that Logan hadn't noticed until now. "I almost didn't."

"What happened? Did something fall on you?"

"No. The man who started the fire hit me. He knocked me out and left me in there to die."

A chill colder than that fateful Christmas Eve in Montana Territory gripped Logan's insides.

"Someone started the fire?" he said.

"Yes. I smelled coal oil and went into the kitchen to see about it. A man I'd never seen before was pouring the stuff around the pantry and the stove. I suppose he wanted to make the fire look like an accident. I realized what he was doing and tried to stop him, but he took out his gun and hit me with it."

And then left her there to die, Logan thought. That would have been nothing less than murder. A white-hot flame of rage began to counter the coldness inside him.

"I guess it was more of a glancing blow than he intended," Vickie went on. "It stunned me. I think I even lost consciousness for a few minutes. But I came to with the kitchen burning around me and was able to get out before the flames spread to the front of the house and blocked the door. It was just luck." She glanced toward the scene of devastation up the block. "Yes, I was lucky."

The bitter tone in her voice made Logan say, "You *are* lucky. You could have died in there, very easily."

"Instead I just lost everything except my life."

Rusty said, "You can start over. You have dozens of friends in Hot Springs, Vickie, you know that."

"A divorced, adulterous woman has no friends," she said.

"I don't believe that," Logan said without hesitation. "I don't believe any of it."

"My husband divorced me. That's a matter of public record."

Logan shook his head stubbornly. "Doesn't mean he was telling the truth about the rest of it."

She stared at him for a long moment. Then she leaned forward and put her arms around him again, this time wrapping them around his neck so she could pull his face down to her and press her mouth to his in an urgent kiss.

Gillian Baldwin had kissed him on the train to Little Rock, but it was nothing like this. A heat more intense than the water from those mineral springs flowed between them. Logan forgot everything else for the moment except the sensation of kissing Vickie Eastland.

Then Rusty said, "I never believed that scoundrel Carleton, either, and all it ever got me was maybe an extra piece of pie now and then."

Vickie started to laugh, even while her lips were still pressed to Logan's. She slid her arms down from his neck and looped them around his waist as she collapsed against him. Logan laughed, too, and said, "I'll bet it was good pie, though."

"It was," Rusty admitted.

Vickie looked up and said, "He lied, Logan. Carleton lied, and so did that man he paid off to claim he'd gone to bed with me. They stuck to their stories in court, and there was nothing I could do about it. I think Carleton must have already reached an agreement with Aaron Nash to marry Elizabeth, because he had one of Nash's lawyers representing him. It was an ugly business, and when I saw what was going to happen anyway, I didn't fight it anymore. I just wanted it to be over with."

"I don't blame you," Logan told her. "But you really ought to try to make people understand the truth."

She shook her head. "I don't care anymore. I really don't. I just want to be left alone to live my life." She looked over her shoulder toward the house again. "And now that's gone."

"It can be rebuilt. We'll figure out a way."

"Plenty of folks'll pitch in to help," Rusty added. "You'll see."

A grim look settled over Logan's face as he went on, "In the meantime, there's the matter of finding the man who did this. You said you'd never seen him before?"

"No, he was a complete stranger to me," Vickie said. "I can't figure out why he would want to kill me and destroy my house."

"Must've been loco," Rusty said. "It'd take a madman to do something like that."

Nodding, Vickie said, "He looked like a madman, leering at me with that awful scar on his face."

Logan stiffened. He reached out with both hands and took hold of her shoulders. "The man had a scar on his face?"

"Yes, like this." Her finger traced a line on her cheek, running back toward her right ear.

Logan realized he wasn't really surprised. There was no doubt in his mind that Jim Meadows was responsible for what had happened here, and he even had a pretty good idea why. Meadows wanted to get Logan off his trail. He must have looked into Logan's life here in Hot Springs the past few months enough to suspect that there might be a link between him and Vickie. Meadows could have hoped that the death of a woman Logan cared for would distract him from the job he was supposed to do for Marcus Baldwin.

Meadows had always been ruthless, but now he had turned into a mad dog, Logan thought.

And there was only one way to deal with a mad dog . .

25.

Logan took his cane back from Rusty. The fear that went through him when he saw the boarding house on fire had made him forget about his crippled condition for the time being, but he knew that wouldn't last. His bad leg might be stronger, but it would get tired sooner than the other one and he would need the cane to get around.

For the time being, Vickie and Rusty would need a place to stay. Logan took them to the hotel and got rooms for them.

"This will go on Marcus Baldwin's account," he told the clerk at the desk.

The man frowned and said, "I really ought to check with Mr. Baldwin about that – "

"I'm on my way to his house right now," Logan broke in. "I'll tell him. If he doesn't agree, he can do something about it then."

Vickie put a hand on his arm and said, "Logan, I don't want you getting into trouble."

"It's too long a story for me to explain right now," Logan told her, "but Baldwin played a part in what happened today. I'm going to ask him to put up the other boarders here at the hotel as well, and I think he ought to loan you the money to rebuild the boarding house."

Baldwin would agree to that if he wanted Logan to work for him in the future.

Even if Baldwin fired him, though, he was still going

after Jim Meadows. The gunman had sealed his fate when he tried to murder Vickie.

The clerk gave them room keys. Logan said to Rusty, "I'm leaving it in your hands to see that Vickie is taken care of."

"Sure, don't worry your head about that," Rusty told him.

"I've gotten pretty good at taking care of myself," Vickie said, the crisp tone of her voice telling Logan that she was a little annoyed with him. He couldn't help that. Now that he had admitted to himself – and to her – the feelings he'd had for her all along, he felt a natural urge to protect her.

But they could work out all of that later, after the threat of Meadows was dealt with.

Vickie drew him aside in the lobby before she and Rusty went upstairs.

"I'm sorry I . . . I never told you how I felt toward you," she said quietly. "Because of what happened with Carleton, I didn't want to trust you. I didn't want to trust any man, ever again."

"I can't blame you for that," Logan said. "Unfortunately, being involved with a man like me isn't going to help your reputation much."

"I think you're a fine man."

"The rest of the world doesn't agree with you. As far as most people are concerned, I'm nothing but a hired killer. A two-bit gunman."

"You and Rusty tried to convince me I was wrong about not having friends. Maybe you need to listen to your own advice."

"Maybe so," he said with a faint smile. "But for now I've got something to deal with."

She studied him keenly for a second, then said, "That

man who hit me and burned down my house . . . you know him, don't you?"

"All too well," Logan said.

"And you're going after him."

"Somebody has to stop him before he does more damage."

Vickie gripped his good arm. "Logan, it took a disaster to get the two of us to say what we've been feeling. Please, don't go off and get yourself killed now."

"I don't intend to, now or any other time." He wasn't going to let himself think about the problems that might crop up in the future as word spread to his old enemies about his condition. Jim Meadows wasn't the only man who wanted to put a bullet him.

One thing at a time, though. Stop Meadows now. That was his only goal.

He leaned down and kissed Vickie again before he left the hotel. His limp had never gone away completely, and it was getting worse again now, the longer he was on his feet, so he was glad Rusty had brought along the cane.

He still had plenty to do before he could rest.

And now that he had thought about it, he wasn't going to start with Marcus Baldwin after all.

* * *

Logan could tell from the guilty start Aaron Nash made that the man was up to something. Logan pushed past Nash's secretary into the timber magnate's office anyway. The secretary was a slender man and wasn't able to put up much resistance, especially with the anger that Logan had fueling him right now.

Nash was standing behind his desk. He reached down toward an open drawer, and for a second Logan thought the man was reaching for a gun. He had brought the scattergun with him, and he was ready to swing it up and convince Nash that would be a mistake.

Then Nash shoved the drawer closed and Logan heard the faint clink of glass against glass inside it. Nash had been getting himself a drink, he realized, even though it wasn't quite the middle of the day yet.

"Here now," Nash blustered. "What's the meaning of this?" His eyes narrowed under bushy brows. "Wait a minute. I know you."

"You ought to," Logan said. "We met at Marcus Baldwin's house a while back. I'm Logan Handley."

"The cripple." Maybe Nash had had more than one drink. His voice was a little slurred. He rested both fists on the desk to steady himself. "What do you want?"

"Tell me where I can find Jim Meadows."

Nash stared at him for a second, then shook his head. "I don't know what you're talking about."

"Sure you do," Logan said as he moved deeper into the room.

Behind him, the secretary said, "I'm going to send for the marshal."

Without looking around, Logan said, "You go right ahead and do that. I can tell him about how Nash's hired killer burned down Vickie Eastland's boarding house and tried to murder her."

The secretary hesitated. "Mr. Nash . . .?"

"Go on," Nash said with a curt gesture. "Close the door behind you."

When the man was gone, Nash continued, "I heard there was a big fire. Mrs. Eastland's boarding house, eh?"

"Burned to the ground," Logan said. "It's sheer luck that she wasn't in it."

"Then she . . . survived."

"She did. That means she can identify Meadows in court. What do you reckon's going to happen when he gets on the stand? You think maybe he's going to say that everything he did was at your orders, Nash?"

"I never ordered him to burn down that boarding house!" Nash burst out. "I never told him to hurt Mrs. Eastland, either." He looked down at the desk and muttered, "Poor woman's already had enough trouble in her life."

"Which you had a hand in. You helped your son-in-law get shed of his wife so he could marry your daughter. You bought her a husband . . . just not much of one."

"You'd think a cripple would have a little more sympathy toward people."

"I don't have time for sympathy right now," Logan said. "Just tell me where I can find Meadows."

"How the hell should I know? The man doesn't keep me informed about his comings and goings! He just shows up when he wants to."

"Then you admit he's been working for you, causing trouble for Baldwin."

Nash shook his head and said, "Outside of this room, I admit nothing. And you'll have a hard time proving anything, too."

"Maybe I'll settle for killing Meadows." Both of Logan's hands tightened on the scattergun. "And if you don't stop trying to ruin Baldwin's operation . . ."

"You'll do what?" Nash challenged. "Come back here and shoot me, just like the bloody-handed gunman you are? I know about you, Handley. You're no better than an outlaw yourself."

Logan drew in a deep breath through his nose. He said, "Maybe I wasn't. Maybe that's changed." He paused. "Reckon it's still too soon to tell."

The menace in his voice was unmistakable. Nash met his level stare for a moment, then sighed and slumped down into the chair behind the desk.

"I swear, I don't know where Meadows is. If I did, I think I'd tell you, just on the chance that the two of you bastards would kill each other. But I don't know."

Logan didn't want to admit it to himself, but he believed that Nash was telling the truth. An uncharacteristic air of defeat had settled over the man. At this moment, Nash was no longer the hard-nosed businessman he had been when Logan first met him.

"If he shows up here, you'd be wise to call the law," Logan said. "I'd say that's your only chance now, Nash. Help stop him before he kills somebody else."

"He hasn't killed anyone," Nash muttered.

"Not for lack of trying. And he's killed plenty in the past. Less than a year ago he tried to blow up a couple of hundred people just to cause a diversion while he robbed the safe in a mining syndicate's office. That's the kind of snake you've been dealing with."

Logan turned and walked out of the office, past the sullen secretary in the outer office, and into the street. Frustration gnawed at his guts. He didn't know where to look for Meadows now, so he supposed he might as well check in with Baldwin and let the man know he'd be paying for those hotel rooms and to help Vickie rebuild the boarding house.

Maybe Aaron Nash would kick in something, too, Logan thought as he strode toward Baldwin's office. It was the least he could do after bringing a monster like Jim Meadows to Hot Springs.

* * *

Nash was reaching for the bottle and glass in the

drawer again when the door opened and Carleton Eastland came in. From behind Eastland, the secretary said, "I tried to tell Mr. Eastland he'd have to come back later – "

"Forget it," Nash said. He waved the secretary away. "Clearly this is my day to be disturbed."

Eastland closed the door, shutting out the secretary, and then turned to face the desk. He said, "Oh, you're going to be disturbed, Aaron. I suspect you're going to be very disturbed."

"We're in the office," Nash said. "Don't call me that."

"From here on out, I'll call you whatever I want . . . Aaron. And you'll call me the new president of this company."

Nash forgot about the drink. He stared at Eastland for a few seconds, then said, "You've gone mad."

"Not really." Eastland walked over to the desk, opened a wooden box that sat on it, and took out one of Nash's cigars. While his father-in-law stared at him in disbelief, Eastland slid the cigar into his vest pocket and went on, "You see, I've been paying attention. I know that Handley was here looking for that gunman Meadows. I know Meadows has been working for you. You ordered him to destroy Devil's Gorge Camp and if I have to, I'll even testify that you told him to burn down Victoria's boarding house."

"That's a damned lie!" Nash said as he thumped a fist on the desk.

"Maybe . . . but I know how effective a lie can be in court if it's done properly. You taught me all about that, Aaron."

Outrage had puffed Nash up for a moment, but now he seemed to deflate again. "So you're blackmailing me," he said. "What do you want?"

"I told you. I'm the new president of the company. You're going to retire."

"Done," Nash said.

Eastland looked surprised. "That easily?" he said. "You're just going to give up?"

"You would have gotten control of the company eventually, since you're married to Elizabeth. Why not now?"

"Well . . . all right." Eastland still seemed shocked that he had won. He said, "And money. I'll need some extra money."

"Now, that's one thing I can't give you."

"Can't – Now, see here! I know how much this company is worth."

Nash leaned back in his chair and laughed. "You don't know a damned thing! I'm in debt up to my eyeballs, and that means the company is, too. We've been on the brink of disaster for months now, and you've been too blind and stupid to see it! The company's only chance of survival was to put Marcus Baldwin out of business. That's why I brought Meadows in and paid him what cash I could scrape up. So, you want to be the president of the company . . ." Nash threw his arms out and laughed again, uproariously this time. "Take it! It's yours, you fool!"

Eastland stared at his father-in-law, aghast. His plans had collapsed. He swallowed hard and tried to regain something, anything.

"I can still testify that you hired Meadows to commit crimes, even to kill people."

"Go ahead, if you really want to send your wife's father to prison. But remember, legally *she's* the one who'll take over control of the company if you do. How much power do you think she'll be willing to give you if you're responsible for me being behind bars?"

Nash saw the despair in Eastland's eyes. His blackmail scheme had fallen apart, and now he was left with nothing.

Nothing but desperation.

He reached under his coat and took out a pistol. It was small, a .32 caliber pocket gun, but deadly at close range. Nash started up out of his chair at the sight of it.

"Elizabeth will be perfectly willing for me to run things if her father is murdered by an intruder . . . say, that hired killer Meadows. If a man like that found you couldn't pay him what you'd promised him, he might lose his temper and shoot both you and your secretary. If I tell the authorities that I heard the shots and ran in here and saw Meadows fleeing . . ."

"You really *are* insane," Nash said. "And you don't have the guts to do it, either."

Eastland lifted the pistol and pulled back the hammer.

Nash tried to rush out from behind the desk. Eastland pulled the trigger. The shot wasn't much louder than if he had slapped the palm of his hand down on the desk, hard. Nash reeled back, collapsed in his chair, and put a hand to his chest where an awful pain had blossomed.

Vaguely he saw Eastland step to one side of the door. The secretary hurried in, drawn by the sound of the shot. Eastland stepped behind him, put the gun muzzle to the back of his head, and pulled the trigger again. This shot wasn't loud, either, but it was enough to send the unfortunate man pitching to the floor on his face as the small caliber slug bounced around inside his skull and pulped his brain.

"You always acted like I was stupid, Aaron," Eastland said. "I was just a show pony you bought for your little girl to cheer her up because she's so ugly. You just never knew, did you?"

Nash made a gurgling sound. His head tipped back slowly against the chair.

He didn't know anything now, and never would again.

26.

Marcus Baldwin was pacing back and forth in his office, obviously agitated about something, when Logan walked in. He stopped short, stared wide-eyed at Logan, and said, "Thank God you're here!"

"What's wrong?" Logan asked. "You've heard about the fire?"

"What fire?" Baldwin shook his head distractedly, then went on, "Oh, yes, I heard something about a fire. A building burned down or something."

"Vickie Eastland's boarding house, where I used to live."

"Good Lord. Is Mrs. Eastland all right?"

"She is," Logan said, "no thanks to Jim Meadows."

"Meadows? That gunman you said has been working for Aaron Nash?"

"That's right. Vickie got a good look at him just before he knocked her out and started the fire."

Baldwin blew out a breath and said, "That's terrible. Why would he do that?"

"I think he was trying to distract me from coming after him. If it looked like the house burning down was an accident, I might have been too upset by Vickie's death to worry about him for a while." Logan's face was hard as stone as he added, "Meadows has a habit of trying to use murder as a distraction."

"Well, somebody needs to do something about the man, no doubt about that, but I have another problem right now and I need your help. Gillian's disappeared."

It was Logan's turn to be surprised. "Disappeared?" he repeated. "What do you mean?"

"I mean she's gone, blast it!" Baldwin wheeled around, snatched a piece of paper off his desk, and thrust it out toward Logan. "My housekeeper found this note from her and brought it here to me. She's run off with that man she's been seeing."

Logan remembered Baldwin mentioning that Gillian had a new beau, but he hadn't really paid much attention and didn't know any of the details. Gillian had probably gone through a dozen different suitors and would likely have a dozen more.

But not if she had run off with the current one. Logan read the note she had left for her father. It explained that she was eloping with the man, who wasn't named, and asked that Baldwin not try to find her. She would be back with her new husband when the time was right, Gillian wrote.

Logan stepped past Baldwin and dropped the note back on the desk. "I'm sorry," he said. "But right now I have to try to find Meadows. Not only that, but I took Vickie Eastland to the hotel. She and Rusty and the other people who lived in the boarding house will need a place to stay, so I told the clerk you'd pay for their rooms. I think you should help her rebuild the place, too."

"Why should I do that?" Baldwin asked with a frown. "I didn't have anything to do with what happened."

"Actually, you did. It was your war with Aaron Nash that brought Meadows here. If the two of you hadn't been feuding, none of this would have happened."

Baldwin glared at Logan for a second, then abruptly shook his head. "All right, that's fine," he said. "I'm as generous as the next man. But right now I have to deal with this other problem. I want you to find Gillian and bring her back!"

"How am I going to do that? I don't have any idea where she might have gone."

A feeling of despair went through him as he realized he didn't know where Meadows might be, either. He and Baldwin were both facing dilemmas they had no hope of solving. They just didn't know enough.

Baldwin must have thought of that, too. He scrubbed a hand over his face and heaved a sigh. "I just can't stand the thought of her running off with that . . . that scar-faced bastard!"

It took a second for what Baldwin said to penetrate Logan's brain. When it did, he stiffened, and his hand tightened its clutching grip on the cane.

"What did you say?" he asked through taut lips.

Baldwin waved a hand in agitation. "That man she's been seeing. She tried to keep his existence a secret, of course. Gillian's always been prone to sneaking around and lying, even when there's no good reason to. But some of my servants have caught glimpses of him, and they told me about him. About the scar . . ." Baldwin gestured vaguely toward his face. " . . . on his cheek."

Logan's pulse hammered so hard in his head it felt like his skull was going to crack open. There had to be other men in Hot Springs who had scars on their faces, he told himself.

But Meadows had always been a ladies' man, able to sweep women off their feet with his charm and good looks and get whatever he wanted from them. It seemed like the ugly scar on his face would have put an end to that, but maybe not.

Maybe Meadows had learned how to deal with what had happened, the way that Logan was learning now.

"Mr. Baldwin," he said quietly, "Jim Meadows has a bad scar on his right cheek."

Baldwin took a step back like someone had just punched him in the chest. "You're sure about that?" he asked in a hushed voice.

"Pretty sure," Logan said. "He got it when a shot I fired creased him."

"My God." Baldwin had to rest a hand on the desk to steady himself. "You think he . . . he's the one who's been courting Gillian? Why would he do that?"

"To cover his bets," Logan said. "Meadows always has to be sure of a pay-off, one way or another. If things had fallen through with Nash, he might have tried to extort money from you to get him to leave Gillian alone. Or maybe – "

Logan fell silent as an even worse possibility occurred to him. Meadows could have insinuated himself into Gillian Baldwin's life in order to kidnap her if his other plans fell apart, as they seemed to be doing now. With Meadows running wild, she could easily be in great danger.

"You don't know that Meadows is the man she's been seeing," Baldwin said. His voice shook a little. "You can't be sure about that."

"No," Logan agreed, "but I've known Meadows for a long time. It seems like the sort of thing he'd do. Either way, I still have to find him. Maybe when I do, I'll find Gillian, too."

Baldwin stepped forward and clutched at the sleeve of Logan's coat. "Bring her back to me unharmed and I'll give you anything you want," he said. "I'll build the

Eastland woman a new boarding house, and she won't even have to pay me back!"

"We'll talk about that later," Logan said. "I have to think . . ."

The only connection Meadows had in Hot Springs – other than Gillian, if he really was the scar-faced man Baldwin's servants had seen – was Aaron Nash. He should have tried harder to make Nash talk, Logan thought. Nash had seemed to be telling the truth when he claimed he didn't know where Meadows was, but it could be that he was a slick liar. Logan's only hope was to go back to Nash's office and try again.

And this time, if it took putting a gun to the man's head, he would do it.

Logan turned to leave the office. "Just bring her back, Logan," Baldwin said. "That's all I ask."

Logan hurried out of the building, and the first person he saw as he stepped onto the street was Rusty Turner. "There you are," the older man said. "Thought maybe I'd find you here. I wanted to make sure Mr. Baldwin was gonna go along with what you said about him payin' for those rooms at the hotel – "

"Yes, and maybe more than that," Logan said. He didn't have time to stop and explain everything to Rusty, so he went on, "Walk with me. I'm on my way back to Nash's office."

While they hurried along the street, Logan told his friend about Gillian Baldwin running off and his theory that Meadows was her mysterious "beau".

"To be honest, I would have thought that Gillian was too flighty to be attracted to a man with a scar like that," Logan said, "but it's possible she thinks it makes him look dashing and dangerous." He grunted. "Meadows fits that last part of the description, that's for sure."

"You think Nash told him to play up to Gillian, to hurt Mr. Baldwin?" Rusty asked.

Logan hadn't thought about that. He considered it for a moment, then shook his head. "I can't say for sure, but to me it sounds more like something Meadows would come up with on his own. I guess we'll have a better idea when we see how Nash reacts to me telling him about it."

"I'm comin' with you," Rusty said. "I don't trust Aaron Nash any farther than I could throw him."

"Neither do I. And you're welcome to come along." Logan paused. "Just don't be too surprised by anything you see."

He heard the flinty tone in his own voice. The cold-blooded hired gunman he used to be wasn't completely buried, he thought.

And that was a good thing, because Gillian might need somebody like that today.

They were nearing Nash's office when a buggy rattled by in the street, moving fast. Logan glanced at it, then looked again. He turned to watch the buggy go around a corner and disappear.

"What is it?" Rusty asked.

"I'm pretty sure that was Carleton Eastland in that buggy," Logan said.

"So?"

"He was in a big hurry."

Rusty shrugged and said, "Maybe Nash sent him to do a job."

"That's what I'm thinking," Logan said, "but from what I understand, Eastland's not much more than a glorified clerk in the timber company. He's Nash's son-in-law, though, so maybe Nash would trust him to handle something more personal . . . like getting word to Jim

Meadows that Vickie didn't die. Nash would want Meadows to disappear. If the law can't catch him, he can't testify against Nash."

"That makes sense," Rusty said with a nod. "Maybe we should follow Eastland and see where he goes." He started to turn. "I'll go back to the barn and hitch up the buggy – "

"We don't have time for that," Logan broke in, "but you can hurry on ahead and have a horse saddled for me by the time I get there."

"You can ride a horse?"

"I don't see why not. And that'll be faster than taking the buggy, since Eastland's already got a lead on us." Now that the plan had formed in Logan's mind, he didn't want to waste any time putting it into action. "Go on, Rusty. I'll be there as soon as I can."

"Well, all right," Rusty said, "but I don't much like the idea of you goin' after Eastland by yourself. What if he leads you to Meadows, like you think he might?"

"Then maybe the two of us can finally settle this without anybody else having to get hurt," Logan said.

27.

Carleton Eastland thought he was rather calm for a man who had just killed two people. In a way, he was a little proud of himself. He was the sort of man nobody had ever paid much attention to. First he was just a clerk and then he was just Elizabeth's husband, and everybody knew that was the only reason he occupied the position in the company he did.

But now he was a killer. A desperado as daring as Jesse James, although if his plan worked no one would ever know that.

He was going to tell Jim Meadows that Vickie had survived and implicated him in attacking her and burning down the boarding house. He would say that Nash had ordered Meadows to get out of the area and lie low for a while. Meadows would want money, of course; his kind always did. So Eastland would tell Meadows that he would meet him tonight and deliver a payoff, money that Meadows could use to put Hot Springs far behind him. That would insure that Meadows would stay in one place for the time being.

Then Eastland would return to town, pretend to discover the bodies of Nash and Teague, the secretary, and tell the authorities that Meadows must have killed them. He could make it sound like he had been aware that Nash was up to something no good but hadn't known any details. Making it all seem innocent on his part, he would reveal just enough to imply that Nash had hired Meadows to cause trouble for Baldwin and kill Vickie, and then he would point the law in the direction of the isolated roadhouse north of town where Meadows and his fellow gunmen spent most of their time.

It was a good thing he had followed Meadows out there one day after eavesdropping on a conversation between him and Nash. Eastland smiled as he flapped the reins against the back of the horse hitched to the buggy. He had acted largely on angry impulse when he shot Nash, but almost immediately, the plan had sprung full-blown into his mind. Since then he had thought it all through and saw no reason why it wouldn't work.

Tonight, a posse would descend on the roadhouse. They wouldn't take chances with a man who had such a dangerous reputation. They would pour lead into the ramshackle old building until Meadows and all his friends were dead.

Then he, Carleton Eastland, would be the hero of the whole affair. Elizabeth would gladly turn to him for comfort and support. She didn't know how to run the company. That would fall to him.

Nash had been wrong. Things couldn't be as bad as he claimed they were. Eastland knew that once he took the reins, he would turn everything around and make the company a huge success. Eventually the Eastland Timber Company would be the largest in the state. After that . . .

Well, there was a governor's mansion in Little Rock that would suit him just fine.

Some clouds had started to move in during the drive from Hot Springs, and a cold wind sprang up. The gathering overcast made everything look even more gloomy as Eastland approached the roadhouse. It was built of roughly sawn planks and sat under the beetling brow of a sandstone bluff that bulged above it. Towering pines grew on top of the bluff. The place had a sinister look to it that was entirely appropriate for the sort of men who congregated here. Human jackals, Eastland thought.

But he could force himself to deal with them in order to get what he wanted.

Half a dozen horses were tied up at the hitch rail in front of the roadhouse, and somewhat to Eastland's surprise, so was another buggy. He had figured he would be the only person out here driving such a vehicle. The buggy was an expensive one, and actually, it looked a little familiar to Eastland, but he couldn't recall who it belonged to or where he had seen it before.

A couple of men stepped out of the roadhouse door as Eastland brought his buggy to a stop. One wore a threadbare brown tweed suit and a derby; the other had a sheepskin vest over what looked like the upper half of a pair of long underwear, and a battered old hat perched on a thatch of straw-like hair. Both wore guns, and the tall, skinny man in the sheepskin vest rested his hand on the butt of his.

"What're you doin' out here, mister?" he asked. "This place ain't for the likes of you."

Eastland knew the man was trying to frighten him. The effort was meeting with some success, too. But he steeled his nerves and said, "I'm looking for Jim Meadows."

"Never heard of him," Sheepskin Vest said.

That was a bald-faced lie, Eastland thought. He said, "I know he's here. If you would, tell him Carleton Eastland would like to speak to him. We both work for the same employer."

Maybe his tone was a little more haughty than he intended. Whatever the reason, Sheepskin Vest stiffened and stood up straighter. His hand gripped the gun butt and started to raise the weapon from its holster as he said, "Do I look like a damn servant to you?"

"No, I just – "

"Then what're you doin' givin' me orders? I oughta – "

Another voice said from the doorway, "That's enough, Cass." Jim Meadows stepped out of the roadhouse and stopped in front of the door. He hooked his thumbs in his gunbelt and regarded Eastland thoughtfully as he went on, "I know you, don't I?"

"My name is Carleton Eastland. I work for Aaron Nash, just like you do."

A sardonic smile curved the left side of the gunman's mouth. "I don't recall saying that I know anybody named Nash."

Eastland shook his head and said, "There's no need to be evasive, Mr. Meadows. I know all about your arrangement with Mr. Nash. I'm his son-in-law and the vice-president of his company."

"Oh, well, then by all means, come on in," Meadows said mockingly. "Sorry we can't offer the sort of hospitality you're used to back in town."

Eastland was getting angry. All three men were grinning now. They were like everyone else. They thought they were better than him. He wanted to take them down a notch, especially Jim Meadows, their leader.

"I didn't come out here for hospitality," he snapped. "I came to tell you that the woman you tried to kill earlier today survived. You managed to burn down her house, but she got out alive and can identify you."

That surprised Meadows. He said, "The Eastland woman's still alive?" He looked even more surprised as something else occurred to him. "Wait just a damned minute. You said your name is Eastland. That bitch is – "

"My former wife," Eastland said. "I bear you no malice for what you did. But now you have to think about your next move. The authorities will have your description soon, if they don't already."

"All right, get down and come on in," Meadows said. He jerked his head at the other two men, indicating that they should go back into the roadhouse.

Eastland climbed down from the buggy and tied the reins at the end of the hitch rail. He said, "I don't see why I have to go inside." Something about the dark maw of the roadhouse's door made him nervous. Anything could lurk in a place like this.

"Because I don't do business standing out in the open," Meadows snapped. "Besides, the wind's cold. There's a nice fire inside."

Eastland nodded and reluctantly followed the gunman into the building. The two men he had seen outside now stood at the bar. Three more men with hard-planed, beard-stubbled faces sat at a crude table playing poker with a deck of greasy cards. A jug that probably had whiskey in it sat on the table; the men must have been passing it around during their game.

The roadhouse's proprietor stood behind the bar. He was short and stocky, mostly bald, with a fringe of white hair around the back of his head and tufts of hair growing out of his ears. He wore a canvas apron that might have been white once but had turned gray with years of wiping greasy, grimy hands on it.

The floor was made of rough, uneven puncheons. Wind whistled through cracks between the wall boards. A pot-bellied stove squatted in one corner, giving off enough heat to keep the chill from being too bad. The air smelled of beer, tobacco, urine, vomit, and unwashed flesh. All in all, it was as squalid a place in which Carleton Eastland had ever set foot.

Which made it all the more astonishing to see the beautiful, elegantly dressed blonde sitting at another table. Eastland recognized her instantly as Gillian Baldwin. The light from the smoky oil lamps that hung from the low ceiling revealed her pale, drawn face. She was terrified, Eastland realized.

"Miss Baldwin!" he exclaimed. He couldn't help himself.

Meadows grinned. He seemed to have regained his composure after receiving the surprising news that Vickie was still alive. He said, "I see you know my other guest."

"You kidnapped Gillian Baldwin?" Burning down the boarding house was audacious enough. Eastland couldn't believe that Meadows had been daring enough to kidnap the daughter of one of the richest men in Hot Springs.

"No such thing," Meadows said. "You came out here with me willingly, didn't you, darling?"

Gillian swallowed and said, "I . . . I didn't know it would be like this. I thought you were a gentleman. I never dreamed you were . . . an outlaw." She looked at Eastland. "You have to help me. You're not the same sort as these men, Mr. Eastland – "

Meadows interrupted her with a laugh. "He's sure as hell not. But he works for Aaron Nash, same as me. He's up to his well-barbered neck in this deal, Gillian." He turned back to Eastland. "Now, what is it Nash wants me to do?"

This changed everything, Eastland thought frantically.

Gillian being here was the worst possible thing that could have happened.

But maybe it didn't have to be. He thought as fast as he ever had and realized that he had to go ahead with his plan.

The only real difference was that since Gillian knew about his connection with Meadows, she had to die, too.

"You're going to have to get out of Arkansas, you and all your men," Eastland said. He made an effort to keep his voice calm and steady. "I'd suggest Indian Territory. There's no real law over there. You'll need money – "

"You're damned right about that," Meadows said.

"Mr. Nash understands that. Even though everything didn't go as planned, he's prepared to pay you two thousand dollars. Getaway money, I suppose you could call it."

Meadows sneered. "Two grand split up between six of us won't get us very far."

Eastland was ready for that objection. It didn't really matter how much he promised Meadows, since the money would never be paid; he was just trying to make the offer sound realistic.

"Very well," he said, sounding grudging about it. "Mr. Nash told me I could go as high as five thousand."

"That's more like it," Meadows said. "You've got the money with you?"

"No. Not even Mr. Nash can put his hands on that much cash right away. But he told me to tell you that he'd have it tonight."

"Then I'll slip into town and see him tonight."

Eastland shook his head. "That's too dangerous. You and your men stay right here. I'll bring the money to you. Say, at eight o'clock?"

Meadows narrowed his eyes. He would have looked frightening without the scar; with it he was terrifying. He said, "Nash better not be trying to double-cross me."

"Absolutely not. I give you my word, Mr. Nash isn't attempting any sort of deception."

That was true enough, Eastland thought. Aaron Nash was far beyond trickery, or anything else except moldering in a grave.

"See to it that you show up with that money," Meadows snapped. "If you don't, I'll hunt down Nash and settle with him. And then I'll come for *you*."

"Don't worry." He had come too far for his nerves to fail him now, Eastland told himself. "I'll be back this evening."

"All right." Meadows looked down at Gillian. "Looks like you'll get to visit Indian Territory. Things over there won't be as fancy as what you're used to, but I reckon you'll get used to 'em." He cupped her chin. "You'll be surprised what you can get used to if you don't have any choice."

Eastland saw Gillian shudder. For a second, a pang of sympathy went through him. A part of him wanted to help her. She was, after all, much more the same class of people as he was.

But more importantly, she was a danger to him. She could ruin everything, so that meant she had to die.

He said, "I have to get back to Hot Springs now." As he spoke, he caught Meadows' eye and inclined his head slightly toward the door, hoping the gunman would understand that Eastland wanted to talk to him outside.

Meadows caught on. He strolled after Eastland, leaving Gillian sitting at the table with her head down.

Once they were outside, Meadows asked impatiently, "What is it now, Eastland? I've already said that I'll do what Nash wants."

"And you've agreed to accept a hefty payment for doing so."

Meadows shrugged. "In this world, you have to expect to pay for what you want."

"In your case, you'll be paying too high a price if you take Miss Baldwin with you."

Meadows narrowed his eyes again. "What are you talking about?"

"Attacking my former wife and burning down her boarding house is enough to get the law after you. But they'll come after you a lot harder if you kidnap the daughter of a rich man. Not only that, but Marcus Baldwin will hire manhunters to track you down, too. He can afford to send the best men on the frontier after you. If you disappear into Indian Territory, eventually the law will give up on finding you. But Baldwin won't. You'll have his men after you for the rest of your life."

"So what are you suggesting?"

Eastland shrugged. "It'll be several hours before I'm back with that money. Use the time to do whatever you want with Miss Baldwin . . . and then kill her."

"Won't that make Baldwin just as determined to track me down? Hell, seems to me like it'd make him want me dead even more."

"No doubt," Eastland said, scrambling to put together a plausible scenario. "But you'll be much harder to track without a prisoner slowing you down."

"I'll think about it," Meadows said with a frown. "It might cause trouble with the other fellas if I took her along and kept her to myself. Of course, we might all split up once we get in the Nations . . ."

"It's just something to bear in mind."

Meadows grinned and said, "Couldn't be that you want her dead because she knows too much about you and Nash, now could it?"

"There's that to consider, too," Eastland admitted.

"Maybe I'll do you that favor. Out of the kindness of my heart, you know."

There wasn't a single shred of kindness in Jim Meadows' heart, and Eastland knew it. He started to untie the reins of his buggy horse.

"But one thing you can count on," Meadows continued. "One way or another, Gillian Baldwin won't be going back to Hot – "

He didn't finish the sentence because at that moment, Gillian burst out of the roadhouse door with the tall, skinny gun-wolf called Cass lunging after her and yelling, "Hey, come back here, you little bitch!"

28.

This was the first time Logan had been on a horse in months, and he could tell that within a mile or two from his aching muscles. He pushed the animal hard along the road that Carleton Eastland's buggy had taken out of Hot Springs. If Eastland had turned off somewhere, Logan would be out of luck. All he could do was hope that Eastland stayed on the same route.

The way the road twisted and turned through the wooded mountains, it never ran straight for more than a hundred or so yards. Because of that, Logan worried that he wouldn't spot Eastland until he was right behind the man.

Providence was with him. He caught a glimpse of movement on the road ahead and hung back. Eastland never glanced behind him as he guided the buggy around another bend and vanished from sight. Logan had gotten a good enough look to be sure the buggy was the one he was after, though. He heeled the horse into motion again, moving even faster now.

When Eastland reached the ramshackle building with the bluff looming above it and stopped there, Logan was just around the last bend in the trail. He could see enough through the trees that came right up to the edge of the road to know that Eastland had brought the buggy to a halt, so he reined in, too, and swung down from the saddle. Carefully, he moved through the trees until he had a clear view of the place.

He watched as Eastland confronted the two men, then stiffened as Jim Meadows stepped out of the roadhouse. If he'd had a rifle and two good arms, he would have been tempted to put a bullet through Meadows' head then and there, just so the man wouldn't have a chance to hurt any more innocent people.

All he could do was wait, though. Armed with the Colt and the sawed-off scattergun, he could fight a battle at close quarters, but not a long-range one.

Before leaving Hot Springs, he had taken off his coat to give him more freedom of movement, and he had strapped the holster Buck Finnerty had rigged for the scattergun to his right thigh. He had discovered that having the weapon there acted as a brace of sorts on his weak leg, making it somewhat easier for him to move around.

Logan's impatience grew as Eastland, Meadows, and the other two men went into the building. He was glad that his hunch about Eastland leading him to Meadows had paid off. But where was Gillian Baldwin? Inside the roadhouse? That seemed the most likely, since the Baldwin buggy was tied up at the hitch rail, too. Was she Meadows' prisoner, or was she still with him of her own free will?

Those questions were answered a few minutes later when Eastland and Meadows emerged and stood talking briefly beside the buggy that Eastland had brought out. Suddenly Gillian appeared, running from the building with one of the other men in angry pursuit.

Meadows moved with the same speed that made him a deadly gunman. He darted to the side and grabbed Gillian as she tried to escape past him. She was moving so fast that her feet came off the ground as Meadows swung her around. Logan heard her cry out. She struggled to break free of Meadows' grip but had no chance of doing so.

That settled it. She was a prisoner. Which meant she had realized what sort of man Meadows really was and what he had in mind for her.

Every instinct in Logan's body shouted for him to help her, but he held back. If he attacked the men in front of the roadhouse, he would waste the advantage of surprise and get himself killed. That wouldn't help Gillian, and it wouldn't bring Meadows and his companions to justice.

If he was going to make a move, it would have to be from close up to have a chance of succeeding.

And he had a glimmer of an idea how to go about doing that.

Meadows turned Gillian over to the other gunman and started talking to Eastland again. While that was going on, Logan heard horses moving along the road. The mount he had brought out from town was tied in plain sight at the edge of the trees. He hadn't thought to conceal the animal because he was in a hurry to find out what was going on at the roadhouse.

Now more riders were approaching, and if they were some of Meadows' allies, he might be in trouble. Even if they weren't, he didn't want the men at the roadhouse to hear the hoofbeats. He turned and hurried back through the trees until he could see the trail.

Logan was relieved – although greatly surprised – when he recognized the three men on horseback. Rusty Turner was the only one who looked reasonably comfortable in the saddle. Doc Reese and Dewey Dumont clearly didn't ride much.

They all hauled back on their reins as Logan ran into the road and waved his good arm for them to stop. Rusty opened his mouth to say something, but Logan signaled for quiet. He motioned for the men to dismount.

"What are you doing here?" he asked Rusty, keeping his voice pitched low so it wouldn't travel to the roadhouse. "I told you to stay in Hot Springs."

"Well, I never was real good at takin' orders, as any man I've ever worked for will tell you," Rusty said. "As for these two galoots – " He grinned and jerked a thumb at Doc and Dewey. "Once I mentioned to 'em that you might need a little help, nothin' would do but for them to come along with me."

"I don't need any help," Logan snapped. "I don't need any – "

"Friends?" Doc broke in. "Is that what you were about to say? Because the way I see it, Logan, everybody needs a few friends now and then, even hard-nosed gunmen."

Rusty and Dewey had rifles across their saddles, and Logan saw the butt of a pistol stuck behind the belt around Doc's ample middle.

"You don't understand. Meadows and his men are all professionals. You go up against them, you'll just get yourselves killed. I won't have that on my conscience."

"You won't have to worry about your conscience if *you're* dead," Rusty said. "We came to back your play, Logan, but we'll be smart about it. We'll handle it any way you tell us."

Maybe they could give him a hand without risking their lives too much. If they stayed in the trees, Rusty and Dewey might be able to pick off a man or two, if Logan could lure the killers outside. The plan he was working on might accomplish that.

"Dewey, can you shoot?"

"I grew up poor," the saloonkeeper said with a grin. "I could knock a squirrel for my ma's stew pot out of a tree at a hundred yards by the time I was six years old."

"All right. Those squirrels couldn't shoot back, though, don't forget that. Rusty, I know you've been in some fights."

"Enough," Rusty said with an emphatic nod. "I can take care of myself, Logan."

"Doc, you'll have to sit this one out with that handgun," Logan said. "Unless things go wrong, in which case, be ready."

"I will be," Doc promised. "You'd better tell us the plan, though."

Logan nodded and said, "Here's what we're going to do."

* * *

By the time Carleton Eastland drove around the bend in the road a few minutes later, all four men and horses were out of sight. The horses were tied deeper in the trees, and Logan and his unexpected allies waited behind some of the pines. Rusty, Doc, and Dewey stayed where they were as Eastland drew even with them.

Logan stepped out into the open and leveled the Colt at the man. Eastland yanked back on the reins and stopped short as he stared down the barrel of the gun.

"Not a word," Logan warned. "If you yell, I won't have any reason not to blow your head off, mister."

"You . . . you can't . . ."

"Sure I can." A grim smile tugged at the corners of Logan's mouth. "I'd even enjoy it, after some of the things I've heard about you. But right now I need you alive, Eastland. Climb down from there."

Confused and frightened, Eastland got down awkwardly from the buggy. Rusty, Doc, and Dewey emerged from the woods and surrounded him. All three of them were as grim-faced as Logan as they pointed their guns at him.

"What do you want from me?" Eastland practically wailed.

"That's easy," Logan said. "I want that fancy suit and hat you're wearing."

The next few minutes were busy ones, too. While exchanging clothes with Eastland, Logan asked him, "How many men are in there?"

"S-six," Eastland said. "Well, seven if you count the old man who runs the place."

"So Meadows and five more gunmen?"

"That's right."

"Where's Gillian in the room?"

Eastland shook his head. "I don't know. Earlier she was sitting at a table to the left of the door. But I don't know what Meadows might have done with her since she tried to get away."

"Has he hurt her?" Logan asked. His face was set in bleak lines.

"N-not that I know of. She seemed to be all right, just scared."

"Fine." Logan settled Eastland's hat on his head. He was a little taller and a little thinner than Eastland, but overall they were built about the same. Similar enough for him to pass as long as nobody looked too closely at him.

Anyway, the masquerade wouldn't have to fool anybody for very long.

"Doc, you're in charge of Eastland. Probably be a good idea to tie him up and gag him. Rusty, Dewey, you fellas know what you have to do."

"We'll be ready, Logan," Rusty promised with a nod. "Wouldn't do any good to tell you to be careful, would it?"

"Not a damned bit," Logan said.

He climbed into Eastland's buggy. He wasn't wearing the holster for the scattergun anymore, but he put the short-barreled weapon on the seat beside him. The Colt was in its usual cross-draw rig, which Eastland's coat concealed where it was strapped around Logan's waist.

He turned the buggy around and slapped the reins against the horse's back. The vehicle rolled slowly back toward the roadhouse.

Logan kept his head down as he drove around the bend. Eastland's hat was the planter type. The brim wasn't overly large, but Logan hoped that when his head was tipped forward the hat would conceal enough of his face. He and Eastland were both clean-shaven, which helped a great deal with the deception.

He figured somebody inside the building was keeping an eye on the road. That hunch was confirmed when the two men he had seen earlier slouched outside. They had come out to meet Eastland before, and now they probably thought they were doing so again. They had to be wondering why Eastland was coming back so soon.

They were close together, always a tactical mistake when facing an enemy. Obviously, they didn't think they had anything to fear from Carleton Eastwood. Logan brought the buggy to a stop no more than fifteen feet from them.

"What the hell is it now?" the tall, skinny gunman asked in an irritated tone.

Logan's right hand drifted down to the scattergun and closed around the smooth wood of the pistol grip. He raised his head and looked coldly at the two gunmen.

They were staring death in the face, and they knew it.

They clawed for the revolvers on their hips.

Logan brought the scattergun up and fired the right-hand barrel. At this range, the buckshot spread enough to take down both men. It blew them back off their feet and dumped them in bloody heaps.

That was a third of the enemy force accounted for right there, Logan thought as he rolled off the buggy seat and dropped to the ground behind the vehicle. He shifted the scattergun to his left hand and drew the Colt with his right as he crouched there.

Yelling curses and questions, two men charged out of the roadhouse. Rusty and Dewey were in perfect position in the trees to mow them down with rifle fire. As the men stumbled and their bodies jerked under the impact of the slugs, Logan thought that this was pretty close to murder. The two hired killers never had a chance.

And how many people had *they* murdered over the years, he asked himself. Any man who lived by the gun knew there was a very good chance he would die by it, one of these days.

The two men collapsed. Just like that, four of them were down in less than thirty seconds.

But now the element of surprise was gone. Meadows and the remaining gunman wouldn't be foolish enough to come charging out like that.

Meadows had Gillian Baldwin to use as a bargaining chip, too.

The ball was started, Logan thought. Might as well call the next dance.

"Meadows!" he shouted as the echoes of the shots died away like the sound of distant thunder. "Come on out, Meadows! It's time we put an end to this!"

29.

For a long moment no response came from inside the roadhouse. Then Meadows called, "Handley? Logan Handley? Is that you?"

"It's me," Logan replied. "Let Miss Baldwin go, and then we can settle this. Been almost a year. It's time."

Logan heard Meadows laugh. "Don't think it's not tempting," the gunman said. "I've thought a lot about havin' you in my sights again. Every time I look in the mirror, in fact."

"It hasn't been an easy year for me, either."

"Yeah, but I didn't do that to you. You put this scar on my face, Handley. And to think we used to be friends."

Breath hissed between Logan's teeth. He said, "We were never friends. Rode on the same side a few times, but mostly not. Now it's over. One of us won't walk away from here."

"I don't plan on walking. I'm driving away in that buggy with this ladyfriend of mine."

Gillian called out, "Logan, don't let him – " before a pained cry ended her plea.

"By God, Meadows, if you hurt that girl – "

"Don't waste your breath on melodramatic threats," Meadows said. Logan could tell from his voice that he was closer to the door now, and a moment later he saw movement there.

Gillian stepped into the doorway. Meadows was close behind her, using her as a human shield as he pressed his gun to her head. Close behind him was the other surviving gunman, looking nervous enough that he might crack and start shooting at any second. Logan didn't want any more bullets flying around while Gillian was where she might be hit.

"I have men in the trees," Logan said. "You can't get away, either of you. Let Miss Baldwin go, and you won't hang. Burning down Vickie Eastland's boarding house won't buy you a rope."

The other gunman said, "I can't risk it, Jim. I'm wanted in other places for worse things. I expect you are, too."

Logan could see only a narrow slice of Meadows' face, but he didn't have to see it to know that Meadows was sneering as he said, "I'm not going to surrender to a damned cripple, either. The girl and I are getting in the buggy, Handley, and my pard here is gonna mount up. You hold your fire while we ride away, or Miss Baldwin dies. I'd hate to put a bullet in such a pretty head, but you know I'll do it if I have to."

"You'll die a second later," Logan warned.

"Maybe, but that won't save her. Let us go, though, and she lives. We'll turn her loose as soon as we get clear enough."

Logan didn't believe that for a second, but the threat to Gillian's life was the trump card. He had expected Meadows to play it, and he had hoped to come up with something to counter it. But he had nothing. He really was a helpless cripple . . .

He stepped out from behind the buggy and set the scattergun on the seat. Standing in plain sight, he placed the Colt next to it, then moved away.

"All right, Meadows," he said. "You want to kill me, go ahead."

"Shoot him!" urged the other gunman.

Meadows looked like he wanted to, but he hesitated. "It's a trick!" he said. "Handley wouldn't just give up his life like that."

"Hell," the other man said, "if you won't shoot him, I will!"

He stepped to the side and thrust his gun at Logan.

Shots blasted from the woods.

But the killer didn't fall. Instead he twisted toward the sound, looking confused. Logan half-turned as well. Those were pistol shots he heard. They had to come from Doc Reese's gun. And he'd left Doc watching Carleton Eastland . . .

Gillian took advantage of the distraction. She twisted desperately in Meadows' grip and ducked her head away from his gun. He cursed and tried to keep her from getting away.

Logan lunged for the buggy and the Colt. The movement drew Meadows' fire. Meadows triggered twice, and Logan felt the hammer blow of a slug striking his body just as his hand closed around the revolver. He sagged against the buggy as pain exploded through him.

The spark had been struck. The other gunman fired at Logan, but the slug tore through the buggy's canvas cover. The man was in the open now. Logan heard the twin cracks from Rusty and Dewey's rifles, saw the man stagger as he was hit. He went to his knees, but he didn't drop the gun. Instead it came up blossoming flame again. Logan called on what little strength he had left and squeezed off a round from the Colt. The gunman's head snapped back as the bullet bored through his forehead into his brain.

Gillian's attempt to get away had failed. Meadows still had his arm around her as he rushed toward the other buggy, dragging her with him. Rusty and Dewey had to hold their fire for fear of hitting Gillian, but Meadows didn't have to worry about that. He sprayed slugs toward the trees as he ran.

Logan did the only thing he could. He steeled himself and broke into a hobbling, limping run and tried to intercept the two of them.

Meadows must have seen him coming from the corner of his eye. He twisted and fired. The slug screamed past Logan's ear.

The next instant he crashed into both of them as he left his feet in a diving tackle.

It was crazy, taking on Meadows like this in his condition. Not only was he crippled, but he was wounded, too.

It didn't matter. He'd be better off dying here if he helped Gillian get away. As soon as she was clear, Logan would yell for his friends to open fire. They could cut down him and Meadows both.

Might as well. They were two of a kind.

The collision jolted Meadows' grip on Gillian loose. She tore away from him with a gasping cry as Logan and Meadows slammed against the buggy. Falling to her knees, she scrambled up again and ran.

Meadows slashed at Logan's head with the gun he held. Logan ducked the blow and tried to jam his Colt into Logan's body. Meadows batted the gun aside and laughed.

"You're gonna fight me? *Me?* I'll beat you to death with my bare hands!"

He smashed his left fist into Logan's face. Logan caught hold of Meadows' shirt front and dragged the gunman down with him when he fell. They rolled toward the hooves of the two horses hitched to the Baldwin buggy. The animals moved around, spooked by all the gunfire, and tried to pull the reins loose where they were tied to the hitch rail.

Logan balled his right fist and sunk a punch into Meadows' midsection, but he didn't think he was able to put enough strength behind the blow to do any real damage. Meadows got an elbow under his chin and levered his head back. Logan tried to buck Meadows off of him, but again he lacked the strength.

Logan hoped Gillian was out of the line of fire by now. Rusty and Dewey ought to open up with their rifles any time. He wished he could call out to them and tell them not to worry about him, to go ahead and shoot. An end to this was all he wanted.

Meadows slammed punches into his body and face with both hands. It took a few seconds for Logan to realize what that meant. Meadows must have dropped his gun while they were struggling. He started to reach out with his right hand and feel around on the ground for it, then remembered that the gun wouldn't be on that side of them. Meadows was right-handed. The gun would have fallen to Logan's left.

He tried to block some of Meadows' punches with his right arm while he willed his left to move. The muscles struggled feebly to respond to his commands. He slid his hand over the ground, felt grass and dirt and pebbles . . .

Then his fingertips brushed against something cold and smooth. The gun barrel. He slid his hand a little farther, closed his fingers around the barrel and pulled the gun closer to him. Meadows was too caught up in the ferocity of combat to pay attention to what Logan was doing.

"Cripple!" Meadows panted. "Damn cripple! Time for you to pay for what you did to me, you weakling!"

"Not . . . too . . . weak," Logan got out between teeth clenched from the strain. He had his fingers wrapped around the gun butt now, but the weapon was heavy, so heavy.

Meadows reached for a fist-sized rock and picked it up. He lifted it over his head and said, "I'm gonna splatter your brains all over the ground, Handley, and you're not strong enough to stop me!"

Logan thrust the gun up between them, driving the muzzle into Meadows' throat under his chin. "Strong enough to . . . pull a trigger!"

Meadows' face dissolved into a grisly pink mist with the roar of the gun.

That took the last of Logan's strength. Consciousness ran out of him like water, and darkness claimed him.

* * *

It was quite a procession that entered Hot Springs late that afternoon, as an early winter dusk settled over the city: two buggies and a whole line of horses, a number of them carrying bodies lashed face-down over the saddles. The group drew plenty of attention.

Logan rode in the first buggy, makeshift bandages wrapped around his upper chest where the gunman's bullet had gone cleanly through him without hitting anything vital, according to Doc. Barber or not, Logan thought the pudgy little man was a hell of a sawbones. He would have bet good money that Dr. August Strittmatter couldn't have patched up a bullet wound with the patient lying on a bar in an Arkansas roadhouse.

Rusty handled the reins of that buggy. Piled into the area behind the seat was the trussed-up form of Carleton

Eastland, who had a bullet wound in his leg. Doc Reese had tended to that wound, too, which was fitting since Doc was the one who'd ventilated Eastland when the man tried to get away.

Gillian rode in the other buggy, which was driven by Dewey Dumont. Doc followed on horseback, leading the horses carrying the six dead gunmen.

Marshal Radcliffe, drawn by all the commotion, met them in the street with several of his deputies. "Good Lord!" the lawman said. "Looks like you folks done went to war!"

"That's the way it felt for a little while," Logan said. "Those men kidnapped Miss Baldwin here. They've been working for Aaron Nash. You ought to be able to come up with some charges against Nash because of that if you want to arrest him along with his son-in-law. We've got Eastland tied up behind the seat."

Radcliffe grunted and said, "I'll put Eastland behind bars, all right, but there ain't a thing I can do to Nash. He's beyond earthly law."

"You mean – "

"I mean the man's dead as he can be, along with his secretary. I'm thinkin' Eastland there probably shot both of 'em. I've got a witness who can put him in Nash's office not long before the bodies were found."

"What witness?" Logan asked.

"Nash's daughter. Elizabeth Eastland." Radcliffe shook his head. "Poor gal's gonna have plenty on her plate. She'll have to take over her father's company, and send her husband to the gallows, to boot! I got a hunch she's strong enough to do it, though."

Logan thought so, too.

Gillian had gotten down from the other buggy. She came alongside the one where Logan sat and reached into the vehicle to take his right hand in both of hers.

"Thank you," she said. "You saved my life, Logan. I'm sure my father is going to be very appreciative."

"That's not why I did it," Logan said gruffly.

She smiled up at him. "I know that." One eye closed briefly in a wink. "But you might let him think otherwise. He can afford it."

"Money won't buy what I need," Logan said. "It can't make me the man I once was, and that's what I'll need to be the next time my past catches up to me. And it will, you can count on that. I was lucky this time."

Rusty snorted. "I don't know what you're talkin' about," he said. "From what I can see, you're a better man than you ever were before you came to Hot Springs. You've got something now that you didn't then, and it'll make folks think twice about botherin' you. You got friends, Logan. Just look around you. You got friends."

Logan swallowed hard and did what Rusty said. He looked around and knew that the teamster was telling the truth.

Then he spotted Vickie hurrying from the hotel, saw her break into a run toward him, and knew that he had even more than that.

He had a home.

Lifelong Texan James Reasoner has been a professional writer for more than thirty years. In that time he has authored several hundred novels and short stories in numerous genres.

James is best known for his Westerns, historical novels, and war novels, he is also the author of two mystery novels that have achieved cult classic status, TEXAS WIND and DUST DEVILS. Writing under his own name and various pseudonyms, his novels have garnered praise from Publishers Weekly, Booklist, and the Los Angeles Times, as well as appearing on the New York Times and USA Today bestseller lists. He recently won the Peacemaker award for his novel Redemption, Kansas. His website is www.jamesreasoner.com.

He lives in the small Texas town he grew up in with his wife, mystery writer Livia J. Washburn.

Westerns By James Reasoner

WEST OF THE BIG RIVER: THE LAWMAN

THE SILVER ALIBI (Judge Earl Stark Western)

ROBBERS ROOST

ROCKY MOUNTAIN SHOWDOWN

RED RIVER DESPERADOES

THE HUNTED

COSSACK THREE PONIES

THE WILDERNESS ROAD

UNDER OUTLAW FLAGS

RANCHO DIABLO:HANGROPE LAW as by Colby Jackson

RANCHO DIABLO: DARK HORSE as by Colby Jackson

TEXAS RANGERS

DEATH HEAD CROSSING

REDEMPTION: KANSAS (Peacemaker Western Award)

REDEMPTION: HUNTERS

REDEMPTION: TRACKDOWN

Non-Fiction

DRAW: THE GREATEST GUNFIGHTS OF THE AMERICAN WEST

Westerns By James Reasoner with L.J. Washburn

RED RIVER RUSE

RIVERS OF GOLD

#1 WIND RIVER

 # 2 THUNDER WAGON

#3 WOLF SHADOW

#4 MEDICINE CREEK

#5 DARK TRAIL

#6 JUDGMENT DAY

#7 RANSOM VALLEY

Mysteries

TRACTOR GIRL Only 99 cents

TEXAS WIND Cody PI Novel

DIAMONDBACK

DUST DEVILS

THE BLOOD MESA

FORT WORTH NIGHTS: A COLLECTION OF CODY PI STORIES

Science Fiction

THE PATHS OF RIGHTEOUSNESS: THE COMPLETE COLLECTION OF SCIENCE FICTION STORIES BY JAMES REASONER

Westerns by James Reasoner and Ed Gorman

THE PRODIGAL GUN

THE MAN FROM NIGHTSHADE VALLEY